CW01099950

THREE FEET OF LIGHTNING

Rita Wilkinson

HAYLOFT PUBLISHING LTD
KIRKBY STEPHEN

First published by Hayloft 2013

Hayloft Publishing Ltd, South Stainmore,
Kirkby Stephen, Cumbria, CA17 4DJ

tel: 017683 41568
email: books@hayloft.eu
web: www.hayloft.eu

ISBN 1 904524 89 3

CIP data for this title are available from the British Library

Designed, printed and bound in the EU

Papers used by Hayloft are natural, recyclable products made from wood grown in a
sustainable forest. The manufacturing processes conform to the environmental
regulations of the country of origin.

*Although the towns and villages named are genuine places,
the characters in this story are pure fiction.*

To my family

*My loving husband Gordon, and my two lovely daughters
Janet and Lynn. An extra special thank you to Gordon who has spent
many hours alone during the writing of this book.*

CHAPTER ONE

It was almost daybreak on a cold and damp November morning on the Cumbrian fells. The forecast was poor, warning of low cloud bringing heavy rain and strong winds by the afternoon, but despite the forecast, farmer Ted Thornton with two farm hands was making the trek mainly on foot up the rugged terrain of the fells to bring down his flock of Herdwick sheep. Over the years he had experienced many such days of bad weather and was aware of the challenges such storms could bring. Nevertheless the three men faced the difficulties in order to bring the ewes down to the farm where they would be joined with the tups to produce next year's lambs. Tupping was the start of the annual sheep farming calendar so the task could not be postponed by bad weather, which was forecast to last several days. The men left immediately after breakfast taking along with them Ted's two trusted sheepdogs Meg and Tess. With everyone prepared for the task ahead they planned to be onto the fells early in the hope that the weather did not deteriorate too quickly.

Ted's great love of farming life on the Cumbrian fells lured him every waking morning, and whatever the weather he welcomed each day with a cheerful smile. His wife Muriel was the first to rise and with the house still in darkness she left the bedroom lights low while she dressed and prepared herself for the day ahead, leaving Ted to rest a little longer until his breakfast was prepared. Lighting up the staircase she made her way to the kitchen where Bess, a now retired sheepdog, was sleeping. Rubbing her cold hands together and breathing into them for warmth she pulled her collar up around her neck and immediately set about getting the Aga back to life to warm the room which was chilly in the mornings.

'By Bess lass, let's get some heat on in here. It's colder than I would have expected this morning. Reckon we will have to turn the heating on soon if the mornings are going to be this cold.' Bess responded with a small wag of her tail but stayed curled up. Muriel knew this would only be until the room was a bit warmer when she would make her way over to her favourite rug and stretch out. The fire seen to, Muriel put the huge black cast iron kettle which had been in the family for many years, safely onto the Aga, boiling the water needed for a large pot of tea for breakfast and a flask for Ted to take with him.

Ted meanwhile stretched himself across the warm, comfortable, bed. He smiled to himself grateful that Muriel would have breakfast prepared for him at the table when the smell of the frying bacon, sausages and mushrooms began to tantalise his nostrils and he knew it was time to get up. After another long stretch he rose effortlessly, washed, dressed and as always looked forward to the new day that was dawning. Muriel's intense love for Ted warmed her heart as she stood at the stove cooking a hearty breakfast to ensure they would both begin the day well. In between turning the bacon and sausages she was buttering bread for sandwiches to be filled with home-cooked ham and mustard, part of the packed lunch which Ted would eat later up on the fell. He wouldn't make it back to the farmhouse until early evening where he would find Muriel preparing him another delicious meal. Regardless of the time he arrived at the table they always ate together to share the day's events. This ensured the farm was running as smoothly as possible by immediately resolving any problems that had arisen, and they would discuss plans for the following day. Spending time together was precious to them both and Muriel seldom took time off for herself. Ted would often suggest, 'Get yourself off for a few hours shopping with Sheila and give yourself a break and a treat.'

Her reply was nearly always the same, 'You know me Ted I'm happiest knowing I am here for you if you should need me and I can get almost everything I want in Pooley Bridge. Fancy clothes don't bother me and when we do need something special I know I can go and get it wherever and whenever I want.'

He could seldom persuade her to take a day off, but he knew what made her happy and the truth behind her reasons for always wanting to be alongside him. He would never pressure her into anything, as to him the most important thing in his life was to see his beloved wife happy and smiling.

As with most farmhouses, the kitchen at Felix Hill Farm was the heart of the home. The welcoming warmth from the Aga with close by the large pine table which was more often than not covered with a clean gingham tablecloth. That morning the salt and pepper pots, sauce bottles, and a half burnt candle, were still in place from the previous evening's meal. The stone floor had numerous rugs of varying sizes, colours and patterns, strategically placed for warmth.

Pictures hung on the painted walls, some of them photographs of their animals past and present, along with many scenes displaying the wonderful colours of the four seasons across the fells. Pots and pans were displayed neatly on metal hooks along one wall by the Aga. Bess had become a familiar part of the kitchen because she had lost her eyesight, and was allowed to spend most of her time indoors. Throughout her lifetime, Muriel's family never kept working animals indoors, and it took some persuading on Ted's part when he suggested it would be safer for her to be inside. Despite her blindness, Bess was still quite young and healthy and they couldn't bring themselves to part with her. As a young man Ted was used to having pets around the house so he loved having Bess indoors. As she lay on the rug waiting for her breakfast, she knew that Ted would be fed first and waited her turn patiently.

The warmth and cosiness of this traditional farmhouse kitchen was the result of Muriel's constant hard work, showing the pride she had in their home. Passed on to her from her late mother, who used to say, 'whilst the men work hard running and maintaining the farm, the wife should be working in the home as well as helping where she can with jobs round the farm.' Her mother would be proud if she could see how much she had followed in her footsteps.

The kitchen door opened and Ted came in and called in his usual cheerful voice, 'Morning lasses,' as he greeted his two favourite ladies, his devoted wife and the ailing dog. Muriel crossed to him and welcomed him with a gentle peck on the cheek.

'Morning Ted how are you feeling this morning? It's a lot colder than we expected that's for sure.'

'You know me Muriel fresh as a daisy and raring to go and fetch the ewes down and the bad weather will not put any of us off.' Bess unresponsive barely turned, knowing Ted would come and give her a pat with his rough hands caused through many years of hard work. Sure enough before he had finished answering Muriel, he was patting her from head to tail, not content with that she rolled onto her back for her stomach to be stroked. 'See you're in your favourite place again lass. Aye you do right, best place to be on a cold morning like this.'

'I'm sorry the bacon and sausage is a bit on the burnt side this morning - doing too many things at once that's the trouble,' Muriel confessed as she put the breakfast onto plates.

'Aye lass I could smell the bacon while I was getting dressed, but no worries you know I enjoy crispy bacon for a change now and again.' Ted was never one to complain and poured the boiling water from the kettle into the extra large metal teapot and covered it with a multicoloured hand knitted tea cosy which was looking a bit frayed around the edges from years of use. 'By that looks a grand breakfast this morning and I see you've added an extra egg and fried bread.'

'You're going to have a long cold day ahead so I wanted to be sure you set off with a good meal inside you.' Putting the plates onto the table they both sat down, then Muriel hesitantly began to discuss the weather knowing Ted hated her worrying about him. 'You have realised the weather forecast is not good for this afternoon?'

'I know that lass but as you know only too well I can't postpone today. Besides Mark has cancelled his dental appointment for this afternoon, and as Stephen's not experienced enough I couldn't risk taking him without his father alongside. It's great the lad has decided to follow him into farming and he's doing really well but he is nowhere ready to do today's job without having Mark along. Who knows maybe next year, should circumstances change.' Aware that the fells could be dangerous terrain and never one for taking risks, Ted knew that should an accident occur, they would be a long way from any of the medical institutions, and sometimes the mountain rescue or the rescue helicopter had to be called to assist. Taking Stephen alone would never enter his head. Mark was also aware of the danger the fells held, especially in bad weather, and was happy to change his appointment so that his son and Ted would not have to go without him.

'My appointment can be changed and besides nothing is going to stop me from being up there on the fells with you both. You know how much I love bringing them down,' were Mark's reassuring words when Ted advised him of the date he had set. Ted, not knowing Mark had made other arrangements for that day, appreciated his readiness to re-arrange his appointment. After rubbing his eyes Ted stretched his arms above his head before patting his slightly full stomach and thanking Muriel for breakfast and all she had done so early that morning.

'You certainly cook a grand breakfast. Anybody going to work with that in their stomach couldn't be anything but satisfied.'

'Well remember what mother used to say? An army can't march on an empty stomach so make sure you feed them well and having helped her serve those extra large portions, it goes without saying I'd be doing the same. She taught me well and you are reaping the benefits from that.'

'Aye for sure she did, she was a good woman your mother, looked after your father and everyone else when she was well enough and always made everyone welcome. The kettle was boiled before you got through the door, even when a nice cold beer or a whiskey would have been much appreciated. That was Margaret though, to her alcohol had its time and place and in its place it stayed, if she thought the occasion was not right. She stuck to her guns, but do you know lass, I reckon she was right about that. Too much alcohol is not good for anybody.'

Bess's ears pricked up. Ted and Muriel knew this was the sign that she had heard Mark's motorbike in the distance. Being blind, Bess's ears and nose were her dominant senses. Her actions warned in advance that someone or something was approaching. Not yet heard by human ears, they were certain that Bess was right and anytime now Mark's ten-year-old slightly rusted Honda motorbike would be racing along the dark farm track, lights on full beam with Stephen sitting pillion clinging on for sheer life. Mark loved to race as fast as he could along the track trying to frighten Stephen who secretly enjoyed the thrill but would never let on to his father.

'They'll be here any minute now,' Muriel commented, and no sooner had the words left her lips than the skidding tyres were heard as Mark yanked on the brakes and the bike came to a sudden stop. The engine faded and he parked the bike in one of the old sheds as he knew it was due to rain before their return. Making their way to the farmhouse they could see the kitchen lights, and knew Ted would be up and ready for them. Muriel greeted them at the door with a cheery, 'Good morning' and invited them in to empty the teapot.

'That'll be a yes thanks for both,' was Mark's immediate reply. After taking off their boots at the door, they hung their coats on the back of the kitchen chairs and put their packed lunch bags beside them next to the table.

'Morning Ted how are you today?' Mark asked while at the same time Stephen was nodding gently, his quiet way of greeting Ted. Mugs filled to the top with piping hot tea, they helped themselves to milk and sugar, and then Muriel left the kitchen to get Bess her breakfast. Knowing she would be fed Bess managed to drag herself away from the rug to follow her into the utility room where her food was kept, a route she was familiar with and avoided collisions. Food and water bowls refilled Muriel left her to eat alone, then returned to the kitchen and spoke with the men before her next job feeding the sheepdogs Meg and Tess ready for their long day on the fells. When she joined the men, Stephen, having drunk his tea asked, 'Would you like me to go and feed the dogs while you have a chat?'

She thanked him, 'That would be a help Stephen it will save me a job this morning. I know it's early but I've a long day ahead of me.' With that he left the table grabbed his coat and went to the door. Coat and boots back on he shouted he would meet the two men at the pick-up then left the house. Crossing to the old hay barn where the dogs slept, he was met by Misty and Smokey the two farm cats who came towards him to be stroked. Seeing Misty had a mouse in her mouth he chose to ignore her and moved to stroke Smokey. Misty was the older of the two and loved to show off when she had caught a mouse or a bird, occasionally she would even parade around the house with it as though to say, 'Look I have done the job I'm meant to do.' If caught, she was immediately chased back outside.

Smokey enjoyed the attention from Stephen but then set off at high speed to catch up with Misty and together they headed for the farmhouse where they would find their food and drinking bowls filled ready. The two sheepdogs spotted Stephen and started jumping up and down as if they had not seen anyone for days. They knew he would feed them as he occasionally did in the mornings to help out, and they waited beside their food bowls like two neglected and starving animals. Several days earlier they had enjoyed a day on the fells with the sheep when Ted and Mark had gone to check if any of the flock had wandered off. Though rare for Herdwicks to stray Ted felt it was wise to check out a day or two before they were due to be brought down for any that had strayed.

Ted and Muriel loved all their animals but had an extra special affection for the dogs. The collies, generally the first choice of sheep farmers, worked hard and needed lots of exercise and mental stimulation - they got more than their full measure as working dogs. Whenever possible they liked to keep one of the bitches from a litter of pups and at that time had three dogs. Meg was the oldest dog on the farm, ailing Bess was her daughter, and Tess was Bess's daughter. Mark and his family also had one of Bess's pups named Tia who was about to have pups herself. Tia enjoyed days with the dogs on the farm when Stephen was up early enough to make the mile and a half walk from Felix Cottage to the farm.

Dogs fed, Stephen hung around waiting until the men left the house for the pick-up which would take all three, along with the dogs to the edge of the fell as far as it was safe to drive. On leaving the farmhouse Ted and Mark said goodbye to Muriel and wished her a nice day.

'Take care all of you,' were Muriel's usual last words as they left the house. She felt the day ahead was slightly ominous but told herself she was being silly, as surely no more accidents could happen to the family. She reluctantly turned to go back into the house and at the last minute glanced over her shoulder for a further look at the two men who were just visible in the dim morning light and watched them as they disappeared towards the pick-up. She heard Ted whistling for the dogs who came racing over and with one leap they both landed heavily in the back of the truck skidding slightly on the damp metal.

Stephen was slightly behind, not having either the speed or the energy of the dogs, and could see Ted and Mark as they threw in their lunch packs and crooks beside the dogs. Ted was the proud owner of the Longstaffe family crook handed down from generation to generation. Mark and Stephen carried shepherd's crooks made from hazel wood for the shaft with crooked handles made from, appropriately, horns from a tup. The sticks were both gifts - Mark's from his wife Sheila, carved with a Herdwick ewe on the handle, while Stephen's was a gift from Ted and

Muriel when he resigned from his job in computers to work for them on the farm. Carved into the handle of his stick was Tia his sheepdog. Stephen, comfortable on an old car seat in the back of the truck, still cold but warmer than bare metal, sat between the dogs. He gave a gentle tap to let Ted know they were all settled and ready to go.

The older men were sitting in the cab of the Mitsubishi pick-up truck, fondly named Mitzy by Muriel. Ted turned the key and at the first turn the engine started. To get a clear view the windscreen wipers swished from side to side, as Ted engaged first gear and they set off on the bumpy journey over the fields to the fell. The excited dogs poked their heads over the sides of the truck, tails wagging as they watched to see which way they would be going. As familiar with the landscape as Ted, they were happy knowing they were off to the fells. Panting with excitement, pink tongues hanging from their mouths, saliva dripping, Stephen tried to keep them calm. He was anticipating his first day on the fells to bring the ewes down and felt slightly apprehensive in view of the poor weather forecast. As he watched day breaking he reassured himself that all would be well, and the decision he had made to work on the farm was the right one. To be outside all day in the fresh air far outweighed the higher salary he was earning working indoors repairing computers for a local company in the nearby market town of Penrith.

CHAPTER TWO

Back at the farmhouse, as she had been up earlier than usual, Muriel decided she had time for a coffee before she went outside to feed the rest of the animals, all of which were part of the happy working environment at Felix Hill Farm. Popping on the electric kettle which she used to boil smaller amounts of water, she chose her favourite china coffee cup decorated with bright red poppies - red was her favourite colour. Adding a teaspoonful of instant coffee, some sugar, hot water, then some cream from the fridge, and with a quick stir it was ready.

Going into the sitting room, she relaxed in one of the comfortable chairs having straightened its red fleecy throw and puffed up the homemade cross-stitch cushion with a picture of a Herdwick lamb which several years ago she had made herself. She stretched her legs out so that her toes were warmed by the heat of the fire which she had lit earlier and, closing her eyes she tried to close her mind from the strange disturbing thoughts she was having. With both hands wrapped around the coffee cup she stared at the flames and smoke that were rising up the chimney, the flickering shades of red, yellow and orange mesmerising her, removing the anxious thoughts as she had wished. Suddenly she flinched as the logs she had added to the fire began to spark, bringing her back to reality abruptly. Bess had followed her and, frightened by the noise of the sparks recoiled quickly, and moved closer to Muriel for reassurance.

'You're a grand lass Bess. It makes me sad knowing you can't see any more,' then she pondered for a moment, wondering how Bess had inherited collie eye anomaly. None of the other dogs as far as she was aware had inherited it and she hoped it wouldn't be passed to Tess or any pups she may have in the future. She could never be sure where it had originated and she hoped that Tia, Tess's sister, who was expecting pups wouldn't inherit the disease. Giving her a quick stroke she assured the dog, 'we will look after you no matter what happens.'

Lost in a world of her own she continued talking to Bess as though she were another human being. 'You know you are special and we will always take care of you. You'll be with us until you're old and grey and all you want to do is curl up near the fire.' Bess as though understanding every word Muriel had spoken, lifted her head onto Muriel's knee for a stroke. Comforting as this was, Muriel was still struggling with an awful feeling that something bad was about to happen to someone or something. Gripping both hands around her coffee cup she took a couple of mouthfuls, curled deeper into the chair then, quite unintentionally, found herself reminiscing of bygone days. Her family had always been happy here at Felix Hill until tragedy struck, then fortunately over the years happiness had returned. Now she wondered had a curse fallen on the farm or family, and if so was it about to strike again? She trembled at such a frightening thought and tightened her grip around the cup as though it could offer her some reassurance.

❧ ❧ ❧

Felix Hill Farm had been in the Longstaffe family for several generations passed down from father to son. The first Longstaffe to purchase the farm from the Barnfather family, who had owned it for many years, was Edgar. Along with his wife Muriel, they had one child, a son they named Harold and he inherited the farm when they died. Harold married and he and his wife Ethel also had one son, named Robert who in due course became the proud owner of the farm. Robert married a girl named Mary Nicholson and they, in keeping with the family tradition, gave birth to a son and named him John, later to become known to all as Jack Longstaffe. It seemed almost expected that with each generation they would have only one child and by coincidence it would be a son who chose to follow their father into farming. This long inheritance resulted in blood relatives of the Longstaffe family still living on the farm.

Sadly Jack's parents, unlike his grandparents and great-grandparents, died quite young and within a few years of each other, meaning Jack had to take over the responsibility of the farm in his thirties. Engaged at the time to Margaret Furness for over eight years, he requested her hand in marriage.

'And not before time Jack Longstaffe. It's just a pity you had to lose your parents before you finally got around to asking. I reckon you never would have asked if we had agreed to Margaret living with you without a marriage licence.' These sharp words were from Margaret's infamously strict father Harry Furness who, along with his wife Ann, vowed that they would disown her should she ever choose to live with him without marrying first.

A quiet wedding ceremony was held at the Registry Office in Penrith with just a couple of friends as witnesses and of course her parents, followed by a simple wedding breakfast at the Water View Hotel where they spent their wedding night. Disappointed their daughter did not want a white church wedding, Harry and Ann had to agree she looked beautiful in her wedding outfit. She married in a pale blue suit with a white chiffon blouse, navy blue accessories and a pretty blue and white bouquet. Understanding it would be difficult for Jack to leave his responsibilities, though not farmers themselves, they offered to stay over at the farm making it possible for the couple to spend their wedding night at the hotel.

The family tradition of having one child was finally broken when Jack and Margaret gave birth to a second child. Their first was a son Michael, born in 1962 then, three years later in 1965 they were delighted when the first Longstaffe daughter was born at the farm. Following several discussions choosing her name they finally decided on Muriel the name of her great-great-grandmother who had been the first female Longstaffe to have her name written on the deeds of Felix Hill Farm.

Muriel had never liked her birth name and that morning whilst sipping her coffee she recalled how, as a child she would grumble to her parents about it. To her it was an old fashioned name to give to a baby girl born in the 1960s and she would often ask her Mam and Dad, 'Why didn't you give me a nice modern name?'

'Muriel's a lovely name,' her mother would tell her, 'it was given to you as a reminder and gratitude to your family lineage.'

After considering her mother's reply she had concluded, 'If that is the reason then Michael should have been called Edgar.' She vowed if she ever had children they would not be called after anyone in the family past or present.

Smiling her mother assured her, 'It is after all only a name, more important is the person you are on the inside and when you are older you will understand that. You are privileged to be alive, and you should be proud that in the future you will become one of the owners of Felix Hill Farm in this beautiful part of England.'

Unconvinced when she was young, Muriel now knew these were some of the truest words her mother had ever spoken to her. Brought back to reality when Bess nudged her, she was surprised to see the time had passed so quickly but refused to allow the feeling of contentment that she now felt slip away. Smiling to herself she slid deeper into her chair and let its comfort envelope her. Her eyes roamed around the cosy room, and with Bess snuggled up beside her she continued to allow her mind to wander to help her escape from the anxieties of the day.

⚘ ⚘ ⚘

Dating from the late sixteenth century, and built of grey stone, Felix Hill Farm with its numerous outbuildings was situated on a slight incline in Martindale, hence the 'hill' part of its name. The farm had wonderful views of the valley and surrounding fells, and also from certain view-points Lake Ullswater itself. The farm was less than five miles from Pooley Bridge the nearest hamlet, and around eleven miles from the market town of Penrith. The house had three large bedrooms, one with a bathroom which Ted and Muriel had installed several years ago, and one family bathroom. Downstairs there were two sitting rooms, one at each side of the hall stretching the entire front of the house and facing in the direction of the lake.

The room on the left of the front door was hardly ever used as it held precious memories, and remained locked at all times as it also contained valuable family heirlooms. Inside they had kept the old style farmhouse parlour with its original fireplace, surrounded by a polished brass fender. It had a cast iron grate hidden by a decorative fire screen of hand embroidered flowers, a rare family treasure. The only modernisation in this room, was electric lighting and a couple of radiators to keep the room dry and warm especially in winter, protecting the antique furniture and family memorabilia, and preventing damp damaging the furniture and curtain fabrics.

Ted and Muriel used the second sitting room regularly in the evenings and at weekends if their workload was not too heavy. Modernised to Muriel's taste it was decorated in creams and red. A red floral patterned wallpaper covered the chimney breast wall while the remaining three walls were painted in a shade of antique cream. The original fireplace had been replaced several years ago with one built from stone and slate. There was a large black metal fireguard with a scroll design on the hearth along with a large coal bucket and a basket filled with logs. Several pieces of furniture were scattered around the room, with old family photographs and ornaments collected over the years, some Muriel remembered were gifts bought by herself and Michael for their parents. Muriel was fond of candles and the room had quite a few on the mantelpiece and coffee tables.

House plants were also in abundance, as Muriel rarely had time to go shopping for fresh flowers. She liked to collect common wild flowers and grasses which she placed carefully in vases around the room reminding them of nature's ever present rebirth. A large three piece suite completed the room where they could relax, watching television or listening to music. Ted and Muriel enjoyed an occasional glass of wine or beer at the end the day, often shared with friends.

The dining room was at the back of the house, but it was seldom used, as the kitchen provided ample room for a large table to seat six. These rooms had been modernised, along with a utility room and small toilet come cloakroom. Facing in the direction of the fells they could see at a distance several of their flock of Herdwicks their faces like tiny white splashes on a painted landscape. The fells and fields in springtime were a carpet of rich greens with the trees an abundance of similar shades. The rocks above, when not covered in moss, were an amazing array of differing shades of greys, browns and blacks. Springtime also saw the fields and fells carpeted in rich shades of green with wild flowers of yellow, white, blue and lilac.

With the summer sun, the rich green is dried into paler shades tinged with browns as the fells burned slightly in a dry year. Autumn brought shades of brown, gold and yellow on fields and trees alike, apart from a few evergreens which maintained their rich colour throughout the year. The cold and grey of winter could make this season dismal if there was not an abundance of sun and snow. In a mild winter, snow could be seen on the tops of the fells, together with the low winter sun, revealing yet more stunning views with the ever changing scenes that the hills, sky, fields, lake and rivers offered.

Muriel had spent the entire 44 years of her life at Felix Hill Farm and had admired year in and year out nature reproducing its magnificent display. How blessed to have had this amazing spectacle of fells, fields and lakes as the surroundings and grounding for herself, and her beloved brother Michael to be raised as children, and for her to still be living here in her childhood home.

⚹ ⚹ ⚹

She recalled how loving her parents were towards each other, to herself and Michael, and to everyone and everything in their care they were kindness itself. Never aggressive even when the sheep tried to escape at every opportunity, leading them and the dogs a merry dance to avoid capture. Voices were seldom raised and they would remain calm until the sheep were all safely penned in with the help of her father's whistling expertise directing the dogs to do their work. They always had time to listen to Muriel and Michael and to give their honest opinion over the choices the children were making, while assuring them both that the final decision rested not with them as parents, but that Muriel and Michael had to choose their own paths to a successful life.

Then of course she thought about Michael her beloved brother and how they had done so many things together. Travelling to school, out walking and sailing, picnics and family gatherings, they were forever the devoted brother and sister. All Michael ever dreamed of was to be an Olympic canoe champion alongside his partner and best friend Philip, and when they had achieved that goal, he planned to return to farm successfully as had all the men in the Longstaffe family. The siblings sat for hours together and talked about how things would be when they were older. Muriel's ambition was to be a veterinary nurse, then should either of them wish to marry they promised each other they could always remain on the farm unless they chose otherwise. Their whole future was Felix Hill Farm and they were confident that after both parents had passed away, together they would continue to manage the farm successfully.

As tears rolled down Muriel's warm rosy cheeks, Bess sensed something was wrong and moved towards her and licked her hand. Realising that she had been day-dreaming for far too long she jumped up with a sudden start, checked the time, and told Bess, 'Gosh I'm running a bit late today lass. I must go and feed the animals they will think I have forgotten about them.' She checked the fire, put another log on and placed the guard around the sitting room fire. In the kitchen, she checked the Aga, grabbed her coat, switched off the lights and, at the same time as putting her coat on, slipped her feet into a pair of waterproof boots telling Bess, 'I'll be back for you later.' She clashed the door behind her and headed as fast as she could to begin the lengthy morning task of feeding the animals.

CHAPTER THREE

It was daylight as Muriel crossed the farmyard at rapid speed almost tripping over Smokey who just managed to duck as she took a leap over the top of her. 'Oops nearly got you,' she remarked and continued to dash first to the chicken coops where there were around 60 Rhode Island Red hens and three cockerels in a nearby field. These supplied sufficient eggs to provide a small additional income by selling to local hoteliers, outdoor centres, tea rooms and shop owners. Having reached the field she opened the coops and hens charged everywhere causing quite a commotion, their wings flapping and yellow legs running at full speed.

As it was November they were locked up in the early evening to be safe from predators and were roosting for approximately fourteen hours each night. It was after 8.30 this morning so they were eager to leave their perches for food and freedom. The various food supplies for the poultry were stored in a nearby outbuilding in tightly closed bins so as to remain dry and inaccessible to unwanted visitors in search of food. Scooping the feed into a metal container she carried the day's supply across to the field throwing handfuls evenly over the ground. Taking a few moments she watched the hens closely as they dashed about pecking, feet kicking in every direction spreading food, grit and earth everywhere, their dark rust-coloured feathers ruffled by the increasing breeze. It was an amusing and colourful scene. The emptied container was used to hold the eggs which she collected from the rear of the coops, counting them as she put them in gently one by one. In spring there would be nearly 60 eggs a day but, as the hens were now moulting, it was down to half that. Crossing back to the farmhouse Muriel placed the eggs into wicker baskets for washing and packing later. She rinsed the container under the tap and returned it to the outbuilding for later that day.

'That's the first job done, now it's time to feed the goat and the ponies.' Muriel didn't realise she was talking to herself, her mind was still a mixed bag of emotions, she had completely forgotten she had not brought Bess out with her this morning, which was part of the normal routine. Her morning had started out so perfectly, but due to the unsettling thoughts, she feared it might be turning into something rather more chaotic.

Rushing around to feed the goat and two ponies, she went to the stables where she lifted a bale of hay by the strings and set off again to the field the ponies share with the hens. The two Fell ponies Lady and Blaze were owned by twin sisters, both horse enthusiasts, but were now being cared for by Muriel. The girls rented the field and stables from Ted and Muriel and attended to the ponies almost every day until they left home for university and with degrees finished, they headed for the city to pursue their careers. The ponies, now mature in years, had lived on the farm for so long Muriel could not bear to see them moved to livery and suggested it would be better for them to stay with her and she would take over the responsibility of caring for them if the girls were prepared to pay for any farrier or vets' bills.

Aware of Muriel's care and concern for the ponies' welfare the girls had no difficulty in making their decision. As the ponies were no longer ridden, their only need was feeding, watering, health checks and grooming, which they got in abundance. Secured by an electric fence, they had their own section of field though they had occasional visitors as the bolder of the hens or cockerels cheekily shared in emptying their feeding buckets and scratched around for spillages.

The one remaining goat named Nancy, also of mature years, shared another fenced area of the same field making it easier to manage them all as one hay bale was sufficient to share between all three. Muriel returned to the outbuildings this time for water. She filled a large water carrier two thirds full which had to be lugged across to the field for filling troughs and buckets. Unfortunately this took two trips as the carrier was too heavy for one journey. It was not the easiest of tasks but she managed to do everything. After a rub and a pat, along with a few reassuring words, the ponies were left to graze. Nancy sadly was not so lucky as Muriel was still wary of her, something which had stuck since childhood. The animals fed and watered she returned to the farmhouse, and on opening the door, she heard the telephone ringing and noticed there were two recorded messages.

'Hello, Muriel here,' she said, picking up the phone.

'It's Paul, chef at Lakes Edge. Thank goodness I've caught you at last. I left a message on your phone but you can't have heard it. We had extra guests at breakfast and are running out of eggs so I was wondering if someone could deliver us at least four dozen before ten. I've promised to do some prep work for evening chef and need them urgently.'

'That's something to ask this morning as there's no-one who can drive along to deliver them. I'm here on my own as the men are sheep gathering from the fell today.'

'We had one person from the kitchen staff not turn in this morning, so it could be difficult for us too, but I'll ask around housekeeping to see if they have time and a car available then I'll ring you back.'

'That would be better for me but if there's no-one available I'll make sure that you get some for ten by coming down with them myself.'

This was something she could have done without. She glanced at the clock and was surprised to see it was already past nine thirty. If they needed eggs before ten then she would have to deliver them herself. She reasoned, the hotel had guests to feed and she only had herself and Bess to think about that morning. Having second thoughts she rang the chef back.

'Paul, Muriel here, looks like you will struggle to get someone here and back again before ten. I'll grab the eggs and drive along myself with them I'll be there as quick as I can and I should make it before ten.'

'Thanks Muriel, as always I knew we could rely on you,' Paul put the phone down relieved and grateful.

'Sorry Bess will have to leave you a while longer I've got to deliver some eggs urgently to the Lakes Edge but will take you out as soon as I get back.'

Luckily there were four dozen eggs already boxed and she put them under her arm. She was still wearing her coat and boots, but decided to change her boots, as she didn't like to drive in them, preferring sensible flat shoes. Rushing back to the kitchen for the car keys from the hook Bess benefited from an additional pat, then she grabbed the door key, locked up and hurried off to the Land Rover Discovery parked in the yard.

Muriel jumped in after putting the eggs on the passenger seat, and at the first turn of the key the engine fired and she was off down the farm track to the main road leading to the hotel. The road seemed reasonably quiet. She passed a couple of walkers and gave them a wave which was reciprocated. Meeting a car coming along the narrow road in the opposite direction, she pulled over to make room and the driver acknowledged her with a wave. She raised her hand and smiled back in return. She hurried to meet the deadline of ten o'clock. A quick left turn into the hotel drive, and the rear of the hotel was facing her. The main entrance was at the front of the hotel overlooking the lake. Paul heard her car and came over to meet her, still wearing his blue and white checked chef's trousers with matching skull cap and white jacket, which now displayed the evidence of a busy morning in the kitchen.

'Morning Muriel, sorry to have had to trouble you like this. I just don't know where all the eggs have gone this week.' He lifted the boxes from the seat of the car, and continued, 'These will see us over for a couple of days until you drop off our regular order. We appear to be very busy again, but we are not complaining as this is what we want. It's good business for everyone all round the area. Will you include them on this week's invoice then we will settle as usual?'

'It can go on to next week. It won't make much difference to me, but if you would prefer that then no problem. Whatever's best for you.'

'I think add it to this week's invoice would probably be better if you haven't already prepared it.'

'I haven't - it's still to do. I was planning on doing some invoices in the next couple of days so I'll do that for you.'

'Okay Muriel thanks, better not be keeping you any longer since you're on your own at the farm today. Hope the ewes are no problem coming down and give my best to Ted and Mark, oh and Stephen of course, nearly forgot him. I heard he's enjoying his work. Take care as you drive back.' Paul closed the passenger door and gave a quick wave before he returned to the kitchen. Muriel reversed the car and set off to restart her daily routine once again.

Her short journey back to the farm was uninterrupted until she turned into the farm track where Chris the postman was just leaving. They opened their windows for a quick chat. 'Morning Muriel, you been out and about already this morning?'

'Yes I've been delivering eggs to Lakes Edge. They've been busy and were running out so I dropped some boxes off for them. How are things with you today?'

'Good, in myself as usual, but with the weather forecast not being very promising I thought I would put my foot down slightly and try to get finished a little bit earlier. Anyway where is everyone not seen anybody about at all?'

'They're up on the fell bringing the ewes down to put to the tups and I'm hoping the weather holds off until they're down. It's looking rather cloudy and dark on the tops already and I can feel that breeze getting stronger, so fingers crossed the dogs do their job well and the ewes are well behaved.'

'To be sure they'll be fine. Ted is experienced on those fells the years he has been going up and down them, and the dogs, well they know what they have to do.'

Muriel gave a reassuring reply, 'Yes they'll be fine, there are three of them this year as Stephen has joined them for the first time so that may speed things up a bit. Better be on my way as Bess has not been out at all this morning. I'm having one of those days where everything started well but now seems to be going haywire.'

'I heard her barking as I put the post through the letterbox but then she usually does if she's in the house. Mind it's always a good sign she's still okay when she tries to warn me off. Well I'd best be on my way.' He wound his window up and sped off down the track to finish his morning deliveries.

With the vehicle parked, Muriel hurried back to the house concerned for Bess and again, having barely made it through the door, heard the phone ringing. This time she ignored it and shouted for Bess.

'Come on Bess let's get you some fresh air and exercise before anything else interrupts our day.' Bess rushed excitedly towards her giving a little bark as though to say 'at last,' at the same time Muriel heard Sheila's voice as she left a message on the answering machine.

'We'll get that when we come back,' she said to Bess, and they headed for the door. Bess made it through first, desperate now for a run around the farmyard and to see the other dogs. Running in the direction of the hay barn to find Meg and Tess, a route she was perfectly familiar with, Muriel shouted to her, 'They're not here today Bess they're up on the fell working. You'll have to wait until later to see them, come on we'll go and see Lady and Blaze instead.' At that Bess turned excitedly in the direction of the field running ahead knowing exactly where to find them. Muriel again glanced at the tops, noticing the clouds getting lower and darker so she hurried in order to finish Bess' morning exercise, feeling she needed to return to the security of the house. After a few runs around the field, with Lady and Blaze looking on, Bess caused havoc among the hens setting them off flapping, Muriel called her and they made their way back.

She realised it must now be getting on for around eleven o'clock, and began to worry knowing that none of the household chores had been done. Even the breakfast table was still laid with the dirty dishes waiting to be washed, and it must be nearly five hours since they ate. She opened the door, letting Bess in first and while taking her coat and shoes off noticed the eggs were still to be washed and boxed.

'Where do I start?' she asked herself, and decided she should listen to the messages on the answering machine first. She listened to Sheila's call asking if the men had got away alright and had Mark or Stephen told her they thought Tia would deliver her pups today, ending the message saying that she would ring back later. Sheila's second call was in a more troubled voice as she was wondering where Muriel was and asked her to ring her back on her mobile as she was at work. Having found her number, she dialed and while waiting for an answer, filled the washing-up bowl with hot water. Sheila answered almost immediately as she had kept her phone in her pocket.

'Muriel at last where have you been all morning?'

'Oh don't ask, the day started off alright. I got the Aga stoked up, cooked breakfast and everything was fine. Mark and Stephen had a quick cup of tea with Ted then they all left in good time looking forward to their day. And, by the way, no-one told me about Tia, but I reckon Mark or Stephen will have told Ted and you know what they're like, they've forgotten to mention it to me. After I fed the animals as I was walking back into the house the phone was ringing. It was Paul from Lakes Edge.' She hesitated briefly before she continued, 'Listen Sheila

I am running so far behind today I have all the baking for the shop and tearooms this afternoon, and a large pile of ironing to do, so why don't you come straight here from work? I'll make us a sandwich and a cup of tea then while we're chatting I can carry on doing my baking or ironing and hopefully I'll get caught up.'

'Your voice sounds a little worried Muriel, are you sure you are alright?'

'Yes I'm OK,' she lied. 'Once I've managed to get caught up with everything then I'll be fine.'

'I'll come as long as you're sure I won't be holding you up. Of course I can always be an extra pair of hands and help you if you will let me, but I know how independent you are.'

'We'll see when you get here I may have got quite a bit done by then.'

'OK, I'll be over later but I must call in on Tia first and see she is alright. I hope to be leaving work around twelve at the latest. We've all been very busy this morning as there's a large school group due to arrive at the centre early this evening for a five day stay.' She thought for a second or two then continued, 'I must let you get on and look forward to seeing you later, bye for now.' Putting her phone back into her overall pocket Sheila was a little concerned by the tone in Muriel's voice.

Brenda, one of Sheila's colleagues having heard the conversation approached her cautiously. 'I don't want to appear interfering Sheila but you sounded a bit concerned, as though something is wrong with Muriel?'

'She says she's fine but I have to admit she was not her usual self - her voice sounded rather nervous as though she was worried. To be honest if she had not invited me over I would have called anyway to make sure she really is alright. Now how much is there left to do as I'd like to get to her as soon as possible?'

'There are still a couple of bedrooms to clean but that shouldn't take us long and, if we are not finished by twelve, then you must leave anyway to see to Tia and Muriel. I can manage what little will be left to finish after that.'

'That's nice of you Brenda but if we crack on pretty sharp we should be able to finish them together.' At that they made their way along to the remaining two bedrooms and, on entering the first which held four single beds, Sheila remembered that when this room was done there were still three sets of bunk beds in the last bedroom. She suggested, 'I tell you what, let's do the bunks first as they are more difficult to make up then, should I have to leave you on your own, you will be left with the easier beds.'

'Sounds a good idea to me let's get moving,' and at that they changed bedrooms leaving the clean bedding on the four single beds until later.

Back at the farmhouse Muriel was worrying she might have cut Sheila off a little short. As she put the phone down for what must be the third time that day she attempted to get some housework done. Having washed and tidied away the breakfast dishes, her next job was the table. She cleared away the condiments and the half burnt candle from the previous night's meal. The red gingham tablecloth needed a wash so she changed it for a white embroidered one. Laying it across at an angle it left the four corners of the pine table uncovered.

Even when she was rushed, she wanted the table to be laid properly. She put two settings of bone china cups, saucers and plates, matching milk jug and sugar basin with two extra plates onto which she would put out the sandwiches and homemade cakes. The white and cornflower blue china tea set had been in the family for years and was no longer complete, so she used its remaining pieces for everyday tableware without having to worry about breakages. Admiring the table she noticed something was missing, and put a small vase of flowers from the windowsill in the centre, and rearranged the flowers to make them look fresher. Happy with the table, she looked forward to sharing lunch and having a chat with Sheila.

She remembered that the bed was still unmade, and dashed upstairs, though why this needed to be done before Sheila arrived was something only Muriel understood. Tidiness was a priority, and on entering the bedroom she picked up Ted's pyjamas from the floor. Why he always left them there she never understood, but she folded them neatly without a second thought. Straightening the pillows and sheets she put their folded nightclothes beneath the pillows. The duvet was shaken until it was fluffed up then spread neatly across the bed. The bed had decorated cushions which she plumped up and put back where they made the bed look comfortable. On to the bathroom - she cleaned the shower, hand basin and toilet, and after checking the towels replaced them with clean ones, putting the dirty ones to wash. She returned to check the room was tidy.

Noticing some dust on the dresser she ran downstairs to get a cloth, and went up again and began dusting the furniture. Reaching the dresser her eyes were drawn to the photographs of Michael and her parents. There were photographs in most rooms in the house but her favourites she chose to have in the bedroom. They were reminders of the wonderful family she so loved and had lost. Picking up Michael's photo she kissed it as she often did and almost immediately was overcome with emotion. Tears rolled down her cheeks and she sobbed, wondering why she was feeling so emotional that day as there was nothing significant about the date. Crossing to the chair by the bed she sat down and buried her face in her hands, and immediately got a flash back to that heart-breaking day some 28 years ago.

'Please God,' she prayed, 'don't let these strange feelings I have had all morning be a premonition that something terrible is once again going to happen to my family.'

CHAPTER FOUR

Both children were born at Felix Hill Farm and Michael was just three when, within a couple of hours of her birth, he met his baby sister. Margaret and Jack having held their daughter for the first time were eager for Michael to see her. Jack had assured his in-laws who were staying to help with Michael, that the birth had gone well and that as soon as the midwife said it was alright they could come up to see their daughter. Michael was pestering his grandparents asking when he could go upstairs to his parents. Eventually Jack called to them and they made their way to the bedroom, Grandma holding firmly onto Michael's hand as, being so excited, he wanted to reach the top of the stairs before he had mastered the first few steps.

'Mam,' he shrieked on reaching the bedroom door. He ran over to her, climbed on the bed gripping the bedclothes as though he were ascending Mount Everest, so eager was he to see his mother and baby sister, he almost slipped.

'Careful Michael,' she said cuddling him then suggested, 'if you sit in the big chair at the other side of the bed the nurse will bring the baby over for you to hold.' That seemed to please him, and after giving him a kiss on his forehead, he jumped back off the bed ran to the chair, and shuffled his bottom comfortably onto the cushion. The midwife took a pillow from the bed and laid it over his legs, then she placed his baby sister onto it so he could hold her gently and safely. His smiling face was a picture as he admired her lovingly. He held her tiny hand, leaned forward and gave her a gentle kiss on the cheek. Looking rather puzzled he turned to his mother, 'What's her name?'

'We haven't decided yet because we did not know whether you would have a baby brother or sister, so we will choose later, but what do you think you would like to call her?'

'Just Baby' he answered eyes wide as though it was the obvious name for her, then kissing her cheek again he indicated he wanted to hand her back to mother. Margaret amused by his carefree attitude looked at the adults and after a little consideration suggested, 'We'd better make a speedy decision to name her, otherwise he may become so familiar with Baby that it will stick.'

'I think you could be right,' Jack replied, 'but not before you have taken a well earned rest will we choose her name.' Taking the baby out of her arms, he placed her carefully into the crib at the side of the bed and covered her over with a light cot sheet, smiling admiringly at how beautiful she was.

Her job finished for the time being, the midwife turned to Jack, 'Well Jack that's another safe arrival. Margaret and the baby are both fine. I've checked everything so I will leave you for today and will be back again in the morning. It will probably be getting onto lunchtime before I arrive.'

'That's fine, and thanks once again. We put it all down to your many years of experience. I reckon you must have delivered a couple of hundred babies around here by now, and I don't think we will find anyone better to replace you when you finally decide to retire.'

'I'll be replaced by a part-time midwife when I do retire. Times are changing Jack with almost all new arrivals being in the hospitals now. Very few mothers are choosing home births and I can't say I blame them when the hospitals are equipped for all kinds of emergencies for mother and baby. Well I must be getting along, I have to go and check on yesterday's arrival, a baby boy near Glenridding. Make sure you have plenty of rest Margaret, any problems just give me a call.' Then smiling she turned to them, 'It has been a pleasure to have been the one to help deliver the first baby daughter into the Longstaffe family at long last.'

Margaret, radiantly happy smiled then closed her eyes for a well earned rest. The bond between Michael and his sister was sealed within those first couple of hours, and every day he spent time protecting her as though he were her very own guardian angel sent to keep her safe from harm's way.

As they grew, Michael began to spend lots of time with his father on the farm while Muriel spent hers with her mother. They knew that one day Michael would have to take over the running of the farm as each generation of Longstaffes had done over the years. Muriel on the other hand, although sharing Michael's love of the farm, was taught from an early age how to run the farmhouse with the result her mother knew that one day she would make some man a good wife.

Both children went to the local infant and junior schools until Michael was eleven-years-old when it was time for him to move on to the grammar school. Throughout those years he looked out for Muriel whenever he could. Having always been so protective towards her he wondered how she would cope with him not being around. What he did not know was that secretly his parents were looking forward to Muriel becoming a bit more independent of him which would encourage her to start developing her own personality. Even though she was only eight when he moved to the grammar school, Muriel knew in her own mind that she had enough friends to manage without him, and like her parents was looking forward to being allowed to 'start to be a grown up' as she called it.

Michael knew he had no choice but to let go and did so reluctantly. Being an excellent achiever academically his parents were very proud when he started grammar school, though he was less interested in achieving high grades as, all he ever wanted to do was be a farmer. His father advised him that there was more to farming than manual work, and it was necessary to have some management skills to run the farm efficiently. Computers were leading the way in business and it would be to his advantage to learn how to use one. 'Who knows what tomorrow may bring, the world is changing fast,' his father told him, 'you must keep up to date in order to survive.'

That last summer before grammar school was spent around the farm and lakes when their parents had time to take them out and about. They enjoyed two weeks with their grandparents at a caravan park and visited some of the coastline and castles of Northumberland. This was the first time the children had been away from home for more than a long week-end, and they had a wonderful time. Their grandparents spoilt them with treats like ice-cream and candy floss but their favourite was eating fish and chips with their fingers straight out of an old newspaper. They had great fun in the amusement parks and in the Hall of Mirrors where they were in hysterics seeing each other in various shapes and sizes. Castles around the area were explored and they hid from each other amongst the ruins, and climbed the towers to admire the views before enjoying picnics in the grounds. This taught them a little bit of Northumbrian history which they both found interesting.

They made several new friends during the holiday and, Muriel became friendly with a pretty girl around her own age named Katy who came from Yorkshire, and they exchanged addresses so they could keep in touch with each other. When the holiday was over they returned to spend the time left with their mother shopping for new school clothes. Muriel had grown out of some of hers and Michael needed the complete grammar school uniform.

✄ ✄ ✄

The morning arrived to return to school and Jack and Margaret were admiring the children in their brand new uniforms with new shoes so shiny you could almost see your face in them. Michael with his hair neat as a barber's model, and Muriel's long blonde hair tied into a pony tail with a green hair band which matched the colour of her uniform.

'You both look like models out of the school clothing catalogue,' Margaret complimented them, 'I'm sure you'll agree Jack?'

The children grimaced and turned to each other raising their eyebrows at the same time, then Michael laughed loudly and said to his sister, 'I don't know about you Mu but I feel dressed like a tailor's dummy.'

Muriel started to laugh, 'I think you look great, besides you'll all look the same,' then elbowing him in his ribs she remarked further about his appearance, 'but none of them will be as good looking as you.'

Flattered, he placed his arm around her shoulders and pulled her towards him, 'I'm going to miss you at school Mu.' Mu was his new pet name for her, which she preferred to Muriel, but they knew it didn't go down very well with their parents.

'Will you stop calling her that,' Margaret snapped.

'But she likes it Mam, and all the other kids at school call her by that name, we think it's cool don't we Mu?' his head nodding and his eyes glaring at her not to disagree.

'Oh you are full of yourself this morning. Okay then, if it makes you both happy and that is what everyone seems to be calling her now...'

Then with a quick glance at the clock she prompted them, 'Come on it's time to move we can't have you late for your first day by missing the bus. Start moving, get your bums off those seats and over to the car.' She passed them their school bags and they both went to give their father a kiss goodbye. Michael however was rather reluctant as he considered he was now too old for kisses. He raised his right hand in the air, his father did likewise and they slapped hands. Jack recognised that his son was growing up. Muriel kissed her father as always and gave him a cheeky grin and, with a smile and a wink from him, she knew he was telling her to enjoy her bit of freedom.

'Bye Dad,' both children shouted as they clambered into the car feeling equally excited and apprehensive at the same time.

The climate was typical for the time of year. The September sun had risen around 6.30am and had warmed the chilly autumn air which Jack had felt when he had first gone outside. It was colder than he had expected and he popped back indoors to get a warm jacket. The cold night air had resulted in a heavy morning dew making everything damp and the car windows had to be cleaned before it could be driven. Margaret, wanting to make sure she could see properly, dried the side windows with a cloth, set the front and rear windscreen wipers on, and honked the car horn. She set off feeling rather subdued. She disliked the children's first day back at school after the long summer holidays and remained silent for the first couple of miles.

The roads were quiet as usual at that time of the morning, and as she drove along the country lanes, she reflected on how lucky she was to have been blessed with two such lovely children. Pulling up at the school gates there were not many children in the playground. They were earlier than usual so Michael could catch his bus. Margaret had expected this might happen so they decided to drop him off first. Driving within sight of the bus she parked the car and nervously watched him. His face was expressionless, he dragged his school bag across the car seat, closed the door, put the bag over his shoulder and left, without even a goodbye. Muriel shouted, 'have a nice time see you tonight.' Margaret remained silent as she thought it was best to say nothing.

Arriving back at the school gates, small groups had gathered in the playground. Leaning over, Muriel gave her mother a kiss, jumped out of the car, slamming the door with the force of a heavyweight boxer, opened the back door grabbed her school bag then ran off into the playground.

Margaret's ears were ringing from the noise of the door banging. She shook her head, then shrugged her shoulders. Driving off she smiled and waved to the parents she knew who were also returning their children for the start of the autumn term. Some, no doubt, would be glad that the day had arrived to get the children out from under their feet, but for Margaret there was a tinge of sadness as she loved having the children around.

She called into the local shop for fresh bread and milk and a couple of other items. There was time for a chat with Debbie who had owned the family run business for several years.

'Morning Margaret, nice to see you. How's the family?'

'Morning Debbie, they are fine thanks, and how is everyone in here on this lovely September morning?'

'Everyone's fine here and, thanks to having a wonderful summer season if the weather keeps up, we should be in for a good autumn.' Then hardly stopping to take a breath, she continued, 'You will be pleased to hear that Gail has been doing very well too.' Gail was Debbie's eighteen-year-old daughter who, with help from her parents, bought the small tea room when it came up for sale. It was a few premises further along the same street, and the family knew the previous owner who was selling up to take early retirement.

'She has had a successful start with the tea room, thanks to Mary delaying her retirement and showing her the ins and outs of running the business. Yes, thankfully we can say we have both had a very successful year up to now.' She paused, 'well enough said about us Margaret, how have things been at Felix Hill since we last spoke?'

'We've had a very good year too. Thankfully we only lost two lambs this season and then shearing went really well. It's a nice time on the farm with all the usual helpers who come along each year, watching them all at work, and the children always have a great time. Michael says he can't wait until he is old enough to do it himself, though which part of 'it' he means I am not quite sure as yet.'

The shop was beginning to fill up, and noticing a long queue forming behind her, Margaret placed her order. 'The usual bread and milk please, a large jar of instant coffee, oh and teabags, the usual large box.' After a long pause she continued, 'I know there are some other things I need but nothing is coming to mind. Never mind I'll make that do, I can always call back in when I come to pick the children up later.' Having paid for her items she put the shopping into a bag then said goodbye to Debbie and went back to the car, thinking about what needed to be done when she returned home. It was around 9.30 when she finally arrived back at the farm, where Jack was waiting patiently for her, keen to know how the morning had gone with children.

'Well how was it?' he asked eagerly.

'They were fine, although Michael was a bit apprehensive and he put on a brave face. As usual I had no problems with Muriel, she was looking forward to moving into her new class but better than that, being able to do what she wants without Michael always appearing around every corner to be at her side.' Putting the shopping away at the same time as talking, she put the bread in the fridge and was about to put the milk into the bread bin when she realised her mistake. Shaking her head at Jack, she watched as he went to fill the kettle.

'I reckon a nice cup of tea is needed to slow you down and to bring you back to reality. There's no need for you to rush around. I'll soon catch up with my work, just doing some repairs today so let's just sit down for ten minutes as you look a bit tired.'

After relaxing for a short while and feeling refreshed she started to plan the day's meals. 'As the children are having a hot meal at school I will just make us a light snack for lunch,' she said to Jack, then laughing added, 'with the bread fresh out of the fridge this morning I can make us a nice cool sandwich.'

Jack laughed with her, 'I'll be back in at twelve for lunch.' He left the house to continue with the maintenance work.

Twelve o'clock soon came and went. The afternoon passed far too quickly and before she knew it Margaret was back on the road to collect the children from school.

'Hi Mam,' Muriel shouted from the school gates, coat flung over her arm and school bag trailing on the floor.

'Hello darling have you had a nice day?'

'Yes it was okay.'

'Would you like to go for a short walk while we wait for Michael?'

'Can we go to Gail's tea room? I'd like a juice and I know you would like a coffee then we can watch for the school bus from the window.'

Margaret agreed and they chose a window seat as it was fairly quiet, and were served straight away. Muriel began telling her mother all about her day at school and how she secretly missed Michael at lunchtime but that she hadn't to tell him!

'Alright that's our secret,' she assured her.

'Here's the bus,' Muriel yelled, then realising just how loud it had sounded, put her hand over her mouth, and looking very embarrassed faced the floor.

'Pick up your things then, and we will head over to the car. Michael will know we are there.' She called goodbye to Gail and they left the tea room. They were in the car before the bus had emptied when they spotted him. He had his school blazer on, but his tie was loose along with the top button of this shirt. Opening the car door he flung his school bag onto the seat then with a lovely grin he cheerfully said, 'It was good.'

That was enough to please Margaret and she headed for home, content that the children were both happy, and that they would spend the rest of their day telling them all about what they had done which would no doubt last throughout the entire evening. Driving along she thought to herself, 'the two young ones will be chattering on all night. Michael will be showing her his timetable, and how much he will be able to teach her when she is old enough to go to the grammar school.'

The night turned out just as she had expected, and eventually, after a long tiring day, it was time for each in their turn to have a good night's sleep, ready to start the same routine all over again the next morning. As the children headed for their separate bedrooms the 'goodnights' were welcomed by all.

Chapter Five

School days were happy times, especially for Muriel who progressed each year both academically and in muturity. It was obvious to everyone that she would get the grades needed to attend grammar school just as Michael had done. Her ambition to become a veterinary nurse never left her. From the age of eight, while she attended the junior school following Michael's departure for grammar school, she showed a greater interest than ever. Even when she was so young when speaking to her teachers she would tell them what she wanted to do when she left school. She was so determined that she spent part of her lunch breaks in the school library with her head deep inside books learning as much as she could.

This sometimes worried the teachers and they insisted that she reduced the extra study to just two lunch breaks a week. The school library was limited in her specific choice of literature and Muriel, not one to be deterred, asked her mother to go to the public library and bring books home for her. From these she learned which subjects she needed to study in order to attain the grades she needed. At the age of ten she worked hard at school and also did additional work at home where, at times, Michael was able to encourage her. Like her teachers, Jack and Margaret found it necessary at times to be firm and take her away from her studies. No-one could fault her determination but the rest of the family, even Michael, felt she needed to find a balance between study and leisure time.

'You are doing far too much reading and studying for a girl of your age, you need to be outside more,' her mother pointed out.

'I know Mam, but I have to study hard to be sure that I will be clever enough to become a veterinary nurse.'

Margaret knew this was true, but there were occasions when she felt her daughter was growing up too quickly, and she was talking to someone much older than ten years of age. Michael advanced rapidly during his first two years in grammar school. Although he was never as keen as Muriel to study he knew he had to work hard in order to please his parents. They often mentioned, that he might like to go to agricultural college, so it was important he maintained his high grades. Michael knew he didn't want to go to college, but kept that secret close to his heart. He still wanted to be capable of running the farm, and slowly realised that he would like to be older before taking over the responsibility.

In the last couple of years he had met and made many new friends at school, who sometimes tried to discourage him from spending so much time helping his father. He discovered new interests and activities, and was about to engage in a sport that would play a major role in his life. His parents had no idea about this, but were soon to find out. Changes in Michael had not gone unnoticed by his parents, and they agreed they would have to allow him more freedom. Michael was Jack's sole helper with certain jobs around the farm especially at weekends. Extra hands were only called in when more experienced help was needed, or to help with jobs too difficult or dangerous for Michael to handle.

Jack's work load was increasing, and with a pair of hands less most days, something had to be done. Financially they couldn't afford to take on a full-time worker due to the increasing needs of the children, and they were finding their money had to stretch further. The demand for children to take part in every opportunity that came along made school costly. They would never say 'yes' to one and 'no' to the other, and there was little chance that any of Michael's clothing or sports equipment could be passed down to Muriel. Things were going to be difficult for a number of years, they were aware of that. They agreed, after several discussions that, as Margaret had the children rather late in her life, and she was not well enough to run both the house and work extra around the farm, something had to be done. They thought that Muriel should help a little more in the house, doing some of the jobs which she seemed to be getting away with, and that would free up some time for Margaret. Jack suggested that they discussed this with the children that evening for an early resolution.

'It's Friday night so they have all weekend to do their homework, and I think it would be better that it is resolved sooner rather than later.'

'I agree, if we are to run a profitable farm then we must all pull our weight. They're two good kids Jack, and I'm sure they will be willing to help, I wouldn't doubt that for a minute.'

'I wish I could be as sure as you, but we have to give them the benefit of the doubt until we have spoken to them and hear what they have to say.'

That afternoon when Margaret went to collect the children from school, she hoped that neither of them would ask to be taken somewhere after supper to spend time with friends as she knew they would be refused on this occasion. The family discussion had to go ahead as planned so that they all understood what would be expected of them in future. Having collected Muriel they bought some food and were just putting it into the car, when Michael's bus arrived. There was no mention of Muriel wanting to go anywhere that night.

'One down one to go,' she thought while crossing her fingers. Waiting in the car for Michael little was said about any plans for that night or the weekend, and Margaret thought it best to say nothing. Walking towards the car with his new best pal Philip, she was sure Michael was going to ask if he could come home with them for the evening and she hated to disappoint him but she knew she would have to. As the two of them approached she thought how handsome her son was becoming, and began wondering if the conversation was about girls' as the smiles on their faces told her something was making them both happy. Philip left and nothing was said, so she concluded they just wanted to finish what they were discussing before the weekend. Michael opened the car door threw his bag onto the back seat as usual, and without saying a word almost crash landed onto the seat. The drive home was quiet but that was normal for a Friday night as they were both generally tired after a week in school.

When they got home, Jack was carrying out some repairs close to the house and said he would join them in five minutes, while the children went straight up stairs to change out of their school uniforms.

'I'll have you both a cold drink and some chocolate biscuits ready when you come down. Oh and put your dirty clothes straight into the washing basket please, not on your bedroom floors.' Margaret was setting the pattern for things to come and caught the surprised expression on

Muriel's face as she looked across to Michael. She could tell Muriel was already thinking it was a strange thing for her mother to ask.

'Guess someone is in for a shock tonight,' Margaret thought to herself as she put the kettle on. Within ten minutes the three joined her in the kitchen and Muriel asked if they could take their drinks to their bedrooms. 'Of course you can but no spills please' she said as they picked up their glasses and biscuits and headed straight back upstairs looking rather bemused.

'I think they have an idea that we have something to say to them Jack and are keeping out of our way but never mind they need to spend some time together before dinner. I'm planning on making it a bit later tonight and then they will have had plenty of time to unwind from school. Is that alright?'

'Good idea, if we make it for eight you will have finished all your jobs and I will make a special effort to be in by seven thirty at the latest and be washed and changed before we eat.'

Margaret called up to the children, 'dinner will be at eight tonight so you'll have plenty of time to do your own thing before then but we would like you at the table on time.' Although she could not see their faces she had a good idea what their expressions would be and what they might be saying to each other. Supper had been prepared before leaving to pick the children up from school so there was not too much for Margaret to do, though there was always, some job waiting in the kitchen. She decided to make their favourite apple crumble for pudding followed by cheese and biscuits. She thought that by extending the number of courses it allowed plenty of time for the discussion.

'Jack and I might even share a bottle of wine and Michael and Muriel can have whatever they want, good idea Margaret,' she said to herself. They regularly allowed the children to leave the table when they had finished eating in order to go and finish homework, but that night was different. They needed to keep them rooted to their seats until they had finished discussing everything and the meal would take longer than normal.

At eight o'clock precisely the family gathered around the table where the first course was ready to eat. Muriel asked, 'Is this a special occasion that Michael and I have forgotten about?'

'It is a different occasion, special in one way because tonight your mother and I have decided that, as you are both getting older, and your lives are changing you need to be included in our discussions about the needs of the farm as well as your own needs.' He filled their glasses with a drink, having already poured wine one for himself and Margaret. He turned to Michael and asked, 'Am I right in thinking that you would like to take some time away from the farm so you can do things with your friends?'

Michael's face reddened, something he didn't often do. Muriel not wanting to embarrass him, as she could see he was not finding this easy, picked up her glass, left the table and took the lemonade bottle from the cupboard and pretended to top it up. She took as much time as she dared without looking too obvious and then returned to the table where the conversation continued.

Michael's head was slightly tilted so as not to have to look his father straight in the eye. He admitted, 'Yes I would Dad. It's not that I don't want to help with the farm, I would just like to have one day each weekend and I don't mind which, Saturday or Sunday to be with Philip and the other day I will help as I always do.'

'Have you anything special in mind that you are planning to do with the day, or do you just want to hang around in Pooley Bridge or Penrith?'

'Well actually Dad,' now he looked straight at his father and made eye contact, and glanced to see his mother's expression, 'Philip has asked me if I would like to start two man canoeing with him as his father owns the Glenridding Canoe Club and is a professional instructor. I can't say I will unless I can promise him that I can set a certain day each weekend for instruction. If we are going to do it, then his father says we must be fully committed. He doesn't want time wasters as he is usually pretty full, and if he is willing to give us his time then I need to be there every weekend. He also said that he would be willing, if time allowed, to bring Philip over to this side of the lake and do some sort of training over here if either of you are too busy to drive me over there. On top of that, because I am doing this with his son, he says he will only charge me half the normal fee it would be for anyone else.'

'Have you thought seriously about this to the point that it is something you really would like to do and could commit yourself to it?' asked his father.

'I have Dad, and you know I have always enjoyed being on or in the water and it seems a great opportunity for us both.'

He looked across to Margaret who appeared to have a rather blank expression. Jack asked, 'How do you feel about it Margaret?' He needed her honest opinion as he thought this could turn out to be an expensive activity.

'If that is want he would really like to do, then we have got to let him give it a try. It would be hard to refuse the offer, especially when Philip's father is kind enough to give him the training at reduced rates. Who knows we may have two future Olympians?'

Michael smiled, things looked hopeful, 'I wouldn't go so far as that, but I know he is a highly recommended instructor and I would love to do it. Philip and I talk about it all the time and what fun it would be but I was afraid to ask as I know how my help is needed around the farm and it will also cost a bit of money to do it.'

'Well this is where you come into the conversation Muriel,' Jack's voice was firm as he turned to his daughter. Startled at the sudden change of attention she made herself more comfortable on her seat and sat bolt upright.

'If you would be willing to help your mother around the house a little, and we are not asking for a full day's work just a little bit here and there over the weekend, this would mean she would have a bit of spare time and has agreed to help me with some of the work Michael has been doing. He could have a day canoeing if that is what he really wants to do, and for you, we would still make sure that Katy comes for holidays and your other friends can come to stay some weekends or evenings.'

She watched Michael's expression and knew he would do it to help her if it was the other way round. 'Alright then,' she sighed, 'but will I get some pocket money for working?'

Jack amused by Muriel's reply twitched his nose at her and answered, 'Cheeky monkey only you would ask.' Looking across to his wife, she smiled at him and he knew her answer.

'Yes I think we could possibly stretch to a small amount.' Not wanting to prolong the serious discussion Jack said that enough had been discussed for one night and he understood the willingness of the children and their future needs.

'Let's leave it there for tonight. We don't need a rule book but let's all promise that we will pull our weight to help each other. It's obvious the farm has to take priority as it is our bread and butter, but equally our individual happiness is important.'

Picking up his wine glass he raised it towards the centre of the table and with his broadest smile and cheeriest voice said, 'Promise?' and they all followed, clinking their glasses and shouting in unison, 'Promise.'

CHAPTER SIX

The family kept their promises to each other and life at Felix Hill Farm ran smoothly for quite some time. Margaret's parents visited sometimes and helped when things seemed to be getting too much for her and Jack, but unfortunately that changed. They planned to move to Lincolnshire to be nearer their other daughter Jenny. They had visited Jenny and her husband Richard regularly in recent months, but because Margaret and Jenny had not spoken for many years, neither of her parents told her what was happening.

Jenny had never been happy that Margaret hadn't pushed herself academically and instead got involved with, 'That Jack Longstaffe' as she called him. She disapproved of Margaret dating him for years, then after he had put an engagement ring on her finger he didn't even arrange a date to marry her. She accused Margaret of being a fool waiting around for him and told her she ought to move on and get him out of her life. The longer the marriage was delayed the more the hostility grew between them, until in the end neither spoke to the other, nor had either tried to reconcile their differences.

Having successfully achieved the 'A' levels needed for the University of Lincoln, Jenny left home to study business management. During the course she met Richard Wilson who was studying accountancy and marketing. They both achieved their degrees and began working for the same international company. Destined, it seemed, to be together, they secretly married and continued to live in Lincoln. Financially they were very secure with success at their finger tips, and they invested well in property and had a home built to their own design. There were no children, so when the company offered them the opportunity to move to the American headquarters for five years, they did not let the chance pass them by. Not wanting to sell or rent out their new home, Jenny asked her parents if they would sell their house in the north and move down to live in their home while they were away. Jenny and Richard advised them where best to invest their money, and when they returned from America promised to give them all the help they needed to buy a home again. It was a hard decision to make but they finally agreed.

This was the reason for the regular visits to Lincoln, and as the time for the house sale approached they explained their plans to Margaret and the family. Everyone was saddened by their decision. The children were particularly upset as they knew they would not see their grandparents very often once they had left the area. Grandma offered that they could visit them in Lincoln during the school holidays. In doing so she was aware of the response she would receive from Jack and Margaret. It was highly unlikely that they would accept such an invitation as the children had never met their aunt and uncle and the family rift had not been healed. The subject was soon closed and never brought up again before Margaret's parents left. The day of the move finally arrived, and Margaret and the children did not see them off as they thought it would be far too upsetting. As expected, as time passed, they saw less and less of each other.

Margaret missed her mother, and although she had never been one to visit routinely, she always knew she could rely on her for help if needed, and Jack missed his chats over a cold beer with his father-in-law. Life had to go on though, and eventually they became used to them not being around. The children were growing up fast, and their lives were so busy that they didn't miss their grandparents as much as they thought they would, but they talked about them regularly.

Muriel continued to work hard at school and to help her mother as promised. Without grandma's occasional help she knew her mother was struggling to keep on top of everything. As young as she was, she could see the pain in her face but was reluctant to talk about it. Instead as she noticed things that needed to be done, she took on more of the household chores, completing her homework later in the evenings, unselfishly allowing little time for herself. She told her parents that she had less homework these days so that they did not worry about her school work, when in fact she would either sit quietly in her bedroom until late into the night or get up early the next morning to make sure it was finished to be handed in on time.

Muriel felt everything was important, and she was determined that nothing would be left unfinished. At weekends she took over the role of cleaning her own and Michael's bedrooms along with the ironing. Their school uniforms were neatly ironed and placed onto hangers ready for Monday morning. She secretly enjoyed housework though she never admitted this to her friends for fear they thought she was strange. When they asked her what she had been doing she generally replied, 'just messing about on the farm,' which could of course mean anything or that she had been with Michael and Philip.

She took pleasure in knowing that she was helping by freeing time for her mother to share some of the jobs around the farm with her father and it made it all worthwhile. On Sundays she occasionally visited a friend or perhaps had a friend to visit her at the farm, but what she enjoyed best was going with Michael to watch him and Philip having their canoe instruction. Jack and Margaret knew that this was not the ideal life for their daughter, but as she never complained they presumed she must be happy. In return they increased her pocket money and on the way to take Michael for his canoe practice they dropped her off at the pony trekking centre where she rode for an hour or so. They encouraged her to have Katy her friend from Yorkshire to stay for a couple of weeks during the summer holidays, or for long weekends at Easter and Whitsuntide. Muriel was never invited to Katy's and the family often wondered why, but they were too polite to ask, and were happy to have Katy.

A routine developed at weekends where on Saturday Muriel helped her mother around the farmhouse while Michael, keeping his promise, helped around the farm. This meant that they had a full day together as a family, albeit a working day, but then they knew that life for a farming family meant working seven days a week, 52 weeks a year. Whenever possible they ate lunch together, then later in the afternoon Margaret and Muriel planned and prepared supper, usually just for the family, but occasionally friends were invited to share the meals made by these two excellent cooks. They could have boasted about their efforts, but it was left to the men or guests to hand out the praise.

Michael looked forward to his day with Philip on the lake and they both took their instruction very seriously. Forfeiting socialising with friends on Saturday nights, except for special occasions, they were happy to stay at home in order to be up early and spend Sunday canoeing. They were dedicated to the sport and Geoff, Philip's father hoped they would take up the sport competitively. He bought a new canoe for their personal use and this gave them even more encouragement to take on the challenge knowing how keen he was to see them succeed. The entire morning was spent training with Geoff, and then they had a lunch break which was shared with Muriel on her days with them. During the afternoon they messed about for a couple of hours while Geoff worked with his other trainees. He then spent another hour with them on further instruction which included all the important safety skills. Always tired after their day's canoeing they returned home happy but exhausted.

✄ ✄ ✄

The weeks and months passed quickly, and Muriel had gained the grades for grammar school. This made things easier in the mornings and evenings for the school drop off and pick up. Margaret felt more and more tired, but tried her best to keep this from the family. However Jack was not blind to this, and began to wonder how he could make her life easier. Money was tight as their outgoings increased, the older the children got, the more the demands became. Muriel, with the help of her father, contacted a couple of veterinary centres in Penrith about the possibility of some advanced training.

Forbes, Mason and Partners, who were the vets for their own animals, offered her the opportunity to spend a few hours each Saturday when, on a voluntary basis, she helped out in reception. They watched to see how she coped with the sick and injured animals as they were brought in. Not being allowed to do this work until she was fifteen she still had a couple of months to wait. In the meantime she researched the career she so longed to follow, using up most of her spare time in doing so. Margaret knew that, like Michael, she was positive regarding what she wanted out of life and that this would take her away from home every Saturday leaving her without the help she relied on. She never discouraged her daughter, but she worried more and more, which did not help her health.

A further problem was on the horizon. Michael and Philip were doing Geoff proud and had begun regular competition runs, but these had to be done every two weeks on a Saturday morning. Geoff saw their potential and set out to train them to an Olympic standard. He was willing to spend the money and the years it would take to do so. Aware that Michael had made great advances in the sport Jack could not hold him back and thought that, as a family, they had to encourage him as much as possible. They bought him a second hand single canoe along with all the necessary equipment to enable him to practice on the lake nearer to home on the lighter spring and summer evenings. This was part of his fitness routine, strengthening his arms and upper body, and also showed Geoff his complete determination to achieve their goal. An old boat house on the edge of the lake near Howtown had stood empty for some time and, after making enquiries they got permission to use it. With a few small repairs and a strong lock it was big enough to store the canoe and equipment. Travelling to and from the lake on his bike saved his parents the job of driving him, and he was now mature enough to go alone.

With all these changes taking place, Jack needed to make a decision about Muriel and the farm which would fit around the children. Margaret's health was failing, and after several visits to the family doctor due to her breathlessness and chest pains, she saw the specialist at the Cumberland Infirmary. The diagnosis was that she was suffering from a weak heart, and was advised to take things much easier and to rest whenever possible. Neither Margaret nor the farm could be neglected - they had reached a crisis that needed to be resolved immediately. The children were very helpful children, even though they were so young. Jack worried with Margaret ill, the family would struggle to run the farm efficiently. The only answer was an extra pair of hands. After several discussions they decided to employ someone to help Jack, so that he could support Margaret. Financially it was not going be easy, but they agreed this was the only way to help Margaret have an easier time.

CHAPTER SEVEN

The vacancy was posted in the windows of local shops and cafés in Pooley Bridge and Glenridding in the hope that a suitable, perhaps local person, would be found quickly. Getting extra help was urgent, yet Jack and Margaret knew that they would have to choose carefully if the successful applicant lived in with the family.

Ted Thornton was a regular visitor to the northern Lake District. He had fallen in love with the area as a fourteen-year-old while on a school activity trip from the North East, and dreamt of the day when he would be old enough to drive across for camping weekends and holidays. As a child he was regarded as a bit of a loner, and his family suspected that when he was older, he would not follow his father and uncles into the shipbuilding industry. He was brought up in the shadow of the shipyard's enormous tankers, among the deafening noise of hundreds of workers going to and from their work day and night. All he looked forward to was the peace and tranquillity of the Lake District, and he longed for the day when he could leave foggy Tyneside.

He left school at the age of fifteen and worked as a second hand car salesman for a rather shady character called Malcolm Brown who traded as 'Browns Quality Second Hand Cars.' He knew Malcolm was ripping his customers off but his personal goal to learn to drive, then buy a second hand car as soon as he was old enough, drew him to the job. He knew he could achieve this quicker working in the car trade. As he had hoped, Malcolm allowed him to drive the cars around the company premises and this gave him the experience he needed to pass his driving test at the first attempt. Ignoring the huge mark-up Malcolm put on the selling price of each car, he worked seven days a week earning as much money as he could by selling as many cars as possible. This pleased his boss who paid him a commission for each sale in addition to his salary.

He bought his first car, a Morris Mini Traveller, from Malcolm who gave him a generous discount and Ted knew that it would not be long before he headed west across the country. He continued to live at home and saved hard to buy good camping equipment for long stays in the Lake District. His mission finally accomplished, he visited at every opportunity until he knew it was time to make his move and resigned from his job. By this time his family had accepted that shipbuilding was as far removed for him as being a brain surgeon was to his father, and that the beauty of the Lake District had stolen him from them.

When he finally left the North East his family were sad to see him go but gave him their blessings. He took on casual work wherever he could, and travelled and visited every lake accepting whatever job was offered to provide enough income to survive. He lived mainly in his car and tent, but occasionally treated himself to bed and breakfast to have a few good nights rest, a refreshing bath and a home-cooked breakfast. He became known around the area as Geordie Ted and because of his honest and friendly character was often offered work through word of mouth. He stayed in the lakes for the warmer months, arriving just before Easter and returning to his native North East for the winter, around late November or early December depending on the weather.

His family were always pleased to have him home and welcomed him with open arms. Equally pleased to see him was Malcolm Brown who was happy to employ him over the winter months when business was quiet. Ted's kept the cars valeted over the winter, especially the ones he was having problems selling, and he carried out maintenance work around the premises. Both men were happy with this arrangement - it provided income for Ted over the winter and Malcolm was able to take time off on the quiet days knowing that if anyone wanted to buy a car Ted had the know how to complete the sale. The winters seemed long to him as he didn't enjoy being back in the North East, and was always eager to return to Cumbria.

He lived this life between the North East and Cumbria for six or seven years. Another spring arrived and, unbeknown to Ted, changes were on the horizon. One day he planned to visit his favourite café in Pooley Bridge, when a local businessman who knew Ted spotted him and crossed the road to let him know about the farm vacancy. 'Would be ideal for you Geordie, get yourself over there as soon as possible and have a word with Jack. He's a grand fellow with a lovely family. It's across the other side of the lake at Martindale. You'll know the area well the time you have spent around here.'

'Aye I'll do that after I've had a bit of lunch, and where would be best to find you to let you know how I get on?'

'Early on in the Bridge Inn, I'm in there every night, you can catch up with me there for a chat, I leave seven on the dot mind and no later. By the way good luck, and be sure to tell Jack that Frank Nelson sent you then he will know you can be trusted, otherwise I would never have put you onto him.'

'Thanks Frank, I'll meet you in there one night as soon as I know one way or the other how I get on, and the drinks will be on me job or no job.'

Ted was not a drinking man and was rarely seen in the pub but made an occasional visit when he had been working and someone asked him to join them for a couple of beers. He shook Frank's hand and thanked him again for bringing the job to his notice, and promised again that he would meet him in the Bridge one night. Arriving at the café, he read the advert in full, while eating a rather large meal of mince and dumplings. The excitement about the job had whetted his appetite. He then went back to the campsite to wash and change and ready, he hoped, to be interviewed by Jack Longstaffe. The adrenaline was rushing through his body, increasing his heart rate, and he knew he had to settle himself down before going to the farm. He took a short rest, read his morning paper, had a cup of tea then, then smartened himself up. Ted saw this job as the opportunity of a lifetime and did not want to fail the interview.

> *Farm Worker Required preferably over 25*
> *Will be working with Herdwick Sheep on fells*
> *along with general farm work*
> *Experience not necessary though some knowledge*
> *of farming would be an advantage.*
> *Live in person preferred*
> *Apply in writing or in person to:*
>
> *Jack Longstaffe*
> *Felix Hill Farm, Martindale,*
> *Pooley Bridge.*

It was two o'clock when he set off for Felix Hill Farm, and headed for the Howtown Road which he knew well. It was a beautiful spring day. The sun shone across the fells which still had snow on the fell tops. The trees were bare, but shades of green were appearing amongst the browns of winter. There was no wind and the lake was spectacular, like a huge mirror reflecting its surroundings. There were few boats on the lake that day, but the Ullswater Steamer was making its steady way towards Howtown Pier. The road was fairly quiet. He passed the odd walker, horse and rider or car, all of which he acknowledged with a friendly raise of his hand. Driving carefully he contemplated his chances of success, and told himself to act natural. The opportunity to work and live with a farming family was almost too much to hope for and he doubted that he could be so lucky as to succeed. He made his mind up to try to be his natural self and to give no false impressions. To be able to work permanently on a farm in the lakes would be a dream come true.

Arriving at Felix Hill he left his car at the end of the road and walked up to the farmhouse. The barking dogs had alerted Margaret and she was at the other side of the door before he had time to knock.

'Good afternoon, are you Mrs Longstaffe?'

She knew immediately why he was there and replied, 'I am, are you looking for my husband about the job?'

'That's right, I read the advert at the café and have called to see him as I am very interested.'

Pleased with his smart appearance, she said she would fetch Jack over from the barn where he was busy working.

'I'll only be two minutes if you would just like to wait here I will bring him straight over.'

Watching her as she made her way to the barn he noticed how slow she was, and thought to himself that she must be in poor health, then allowing his eyes to rove around the farmyard he thought how much he would love living and working in a place like this. Jack arrived within minutes and greeted him, 'Good afternoon young man, nice to meet you.' The two men shook hands firmly and Ted introduced himself.

'Nice to meet you too Mr Longstaffe and of course your good lady,' and turning to Margaret he gave her a friendly smile.

'Jack's the name and my wife is Margaret, nothing formal around here - first name terms only.'

'Edward Thornton known as Ted, though I'm better known around here as Geordie Ted.'

'I thought I recognised that accent, a North East lad eh? So what brings you to these parts - looking for work?'

Margaret suggested they go into the house and offered to make a pot of tea. Ted realised that an interview over a cup of tea, on first name terms, was not going to be too formal, and allowed himself to relax slightly.

'I fell in love with this area as a lad of fourteen on a week's visit here with school and vowed I would return as soon as I was old enough to leave the nest. I live over here for eight to nine months of the year and have been doing so since I was coming on nineteen. I go home only to fill in the winter months when there is little work about, and of course to see my family. All the men in my family are shipbuilders but that work wouldn't have suited me.'

'Your family would be disappointed were they, when you didn't follow them into the shipyards?'

'Aye they were that, but a lad has to follow his own instinct and mine was to live here with the peace and quiet with plenty of good clean healthy air to fill my lungs.'

'Well good thing you stuck your ground. I can't say I blame you. This is a wonderful place to live and work, been here all my life. By the way can I ask where did you spot the advert?'

'I didn't at first. Frank Nelson pointed it out as I was heading for the café. He spotted me and knew I would be interested and didn't want me to miss the opportunity. He said I'd to tell you that it was him who sent me along.'

'Grand fellow is Frank, and that makes for a good start as I know he would not send anyone unsuitable or untrustworthy. We have known each other for many a year and he would know the type of person we are looking for.'

Margaret had made the tea and came to the table with two large mugs, milk, sugar and some chocolate biscuits. She said she prefered the men to discuss the vacancy without her, and headed back to the sitting room where she had been taking an afternoon rest before Ted arrived. Jack passed a mug across the table and began to ask about Ted's past. 'Help yourself to tea and biscuits, and then let's find out a bit about you - what work you have done, and why you would like to come to work for us here.'

'Well, I'm 25 now. I left school at fifteen and worked as a car salesman for a few years, and that helped me save to buy a decent little car, which was what I wanted to do so that I could come over to the lakes for weekends and holidays. In time I decided to live over here during the summer season and, by camping out and doing casual work wherever I could get it I knew I would survive. At first I travelled around the lakes until I decided where I wanted to settle, then after the first couple of years I chose the Ullswater area and have been very lucky.

'After coming here for a few years now, lots of people know me and offer me work year in and year out. I've worked in kitchens, waited on in bars and hotels, and done maintenance work at the boat clubs and campsites, in fact I've done all sorts. But obviously you will be wondering if I have done anything on the farms around here, well I can tell you 'yes' to that one too, and that is why I'm here. I've done various jobs on farms across Cumbria, working with sheep and cattle and done lots of maintenance work. I've even helped the lads with a bit of dry stone walling now and again.'

'Sounds to me that you can turn a hand to most things then?'

'That I can assure you, and I'll always have a good try at anything. I've never turned down any job I have been offered and never been sacked from one either. I give of my best to earn my pay.'

Jack continued by explaining in detail why he planned to employ someone, and the reason he prefered to have them live in. 'We need to keep expenses down as much as possible. The children are eating up a lot more of our income these days and we felt if we supplied food and accommodation then this could reduce the weekly wage we would have to pay, as board and lodgings would be taken into consideration regarding the salary we could offer.'

'Sounds fine to me Jack, I wouldn't have a problem with that as long as I have enough money to be able to save a little so I can visit my family every now and again.'

'Another thing that's important and you need to know beforehand is that we will need you to work not only on the farm, but to be willing to help out in other ways too. You see Margaret's health is deteriorating and, with the children needing transporting here there and everywhere, we could do with someone who would be prepared to taxi them around if we weren't able to, and even be willing to collect a few items of shopping maybe, whilst out and about.'

'I would do whatever I'm asked. To be able to work here and live with the family would be my ultimate dream. I realise that you will need references from past employers, and I can give you contact numbers right now so you get them straightaway if you were to consider me for the job.'

'Tell you what Ted, Margaret is due to go off for the children soon, so I'll call her in as she will be wondering how it's going.' He opened the door and gave Margaret a nod and a wink to say that, up to now, he was pleased. 'Margaret, I need you to come and join us as we agreed it would be a joint decision as to who we employ.' They sat around the table and Jack assured both Margaret and Ted he was happy with how the interview had gone so far, and asked Margaret if there was anything specific she would like to ask.

'Jack will have told you we have two teenage children both at grammar school. Michael is seventeen and Muriel is fourteen, and their lives are now taken up with school, homework and hobbies. It's because of this they are not able to help us as much as they used to, so we need someone to take over some of the jobs Michael does with his father, in order to free Jack up for other things as my health is not good and I don't have the energy to work like I used to. One thing we wouldn't want is someone who would resent the children doing their own thing.'

'I assure you Mrs Longstaffe, sorry Margaret, I was a teenager myself not long ago, and they have to have their freedom in order to discover what they really want out of life. My family wanted me to be a shipbuilder but I went my own way, and that's why I'm sitting here today.'

The more the conversation continued, the more Jack and Margaret liked the young man. Jack looked across to Margaret and asked, 'What do you say Margaret? Should Ted stay here and I'll show him around the farm while you go and pick the children up from school? Then we could have some tea together so they can meet him and see where we go from there?'

'Sounds a good idea to me. I'll be off and will leave you both to it and will get back home as quickly as I can.'

An hour or so later they were around the table again, this time with the children. Over a cup of tea, ham sandwiches and fruit cake, they got along well. Michael was buzzing, telling Ted about his canoeing while Muriel kept trying without success to get a word in as she wanted to tell Ted what she planned to do when she left school. They were getting along so well it seemed too good to be true.

The time passed quickly and as the children had homework Jack stepped in. 'I think we should leave it for today as we need to discuss this as a family before we make any decisions. If it's alright with you, I'll get back to you as soon as possible, or if you would like to ring me in a couple of days when we've decided I can let you know. I'll have your references checked out tomorrow if they are needed, and providing they are good you would then be able to start as soon as everything is arranged possibly the 1st of April - that's the date I had in mind.'

Ted shook hands with Jack, Margaret and Michael, but Muriel headed off to her bedroom with a simple, 'Bye Ted.'

'I'll ring you in a couple of days then, when do you suggest is the best time to call?'

'Around eight o'clock, evening that is, then one of us is sure to be near the phone. Thanks for coming over Ted and hopefully we will see you again soon.'

Making his way back to the car Ted felt like running, he had such a good feeling about the way things had gone. 'Well Ted Thornton only a couple of days and you'll know for sure. I bet these will be two of the longest days of my life as I'd like this job so much.' Still talking to himself he got into the car, started the engine, turned the car and put his foot down hard on the accelerator. He headed back towards Pooley Bridge travelling at twice the speed he did on the journey into Martindale.

CHAPTER EIGHT

Ted's family didn't understand how he loved his life under canvas so much but, as he was happy and healthy when he returned home, they accepted it. After all, his mother would tell herself, he was a good son who had never intentionally brought any trouble to their doorstep. His parents were worried about his love of his own company, and they expected that, once he started work, he would mix more with people of his own age, but he never did. Accepting that he had his own ideas about what he wanted from life they resigned themselves to not trying to change him. When he was about to take on a permanent job on a lonely sheep farm in Cumbria, his mother's concerns increased.

'Look at him now, 25 years of age and still no females in his life as far as we are aware, and now he is off to look after sheep in the middle of nowhere on the lonely Cumbrian fells. Some chance of him meeting a woman there!' She was becoming agitated and mumbled away to her husband who seemed to take little notice as he found the morning news-paper far more interesting.

'He'll end up a lonely old bachelor and what will happen to him when we are no longer around to offer him a comfortable home when he needs one? The thing is he needs a good wife who will be there to look after him, like I have done for you for nearly 30 years. Not that you have ever given me much praise for all I've done for the family. Not as much as a thank you from you unless you have a few beers down your neck.'

Throwing the paper across the room, he was angry with her and snapped, 'For goodness sake woman will you stop fretting over that lad. He's a grown man who has made his own mind up and it's nowt to do with us what he does with his life. He chose it and he will have to accept whatever happens to him in the future. He has always been an oddball, brought shame to this family not wanting to follow us men into the ship-yards. For generations all the men in the Thornton family worked in the shipyards and it would never have even been considered to do anything different. We're shipbuilders to the core in these parts, which makes me wonder what stock the lad comes from because he's nowt like the fellas on my side of the family.'

'That's enough of that from you Robert Thornton. The men in my family are all good grafters and they also know how to look after their womenfolk properly. There's no oddballs in the Armstrong family so he obviously must take after somebody from your side.'

His face red with rage, he shouted, 'For goodness sake woman will you drop it? Let him get on with it. He knew he let us fellas down when he made his ridiculous choice and we'll never let him forget it either. Trouble with him is he's afraid of a bit of hard graft and shift work. Me and our lad will never forget how that lot down the yard gave us some stick when they heard he was going off to sell cars when he left school.'

'Maybe they did go on a bit but no-one can deny he worked bloody long hard hours for Malcolm Brown and you can't fault him for that.'

'You can cut that language out Mrs T. It's not like you to swear but I tell you I'll never forget the sarcastic remarks the lads threw at me over a pint of Newcastle Brown down at the pub. 'What kind of a son is that you've bred?' or 'He's not going to turn into much of a man is he?''

Recalling the nights he had returned home worse for wear after several pints, she reminded him of how it really had been. 'Shouldn't that be over a few pints of Newcastle Brown. It'll be a first when you go down to the pub and have just one.'

He ignored her remark, as he didn't want a full blown row, he continued, 'Aye things got close to a fight in the bar many a time when someone wouldn't let the matter drop. I'd lose me temper pretty quick and seeing me taking me jacket off and pushing me sleeves up one of the lads would immediately step in to stop it before it turned into a brawl.'

'Well those days are behind us now and people forget and move on. You'll not admit it, but I know you are looking forward to him arriving for a short visit before he goes off to start this new job. Come to think of it this will be the first full-time job he has had since leaving Malcolm's place.'

'Aye now there's a thought. I'd not looked at it like that before, but guess you might be right. It's no use holding grudges. At least he fends for himself and asks nowt from us other than a comfortable bed and a few decent meals when he's here.'

Ted arrived for his visit and his parents were pleased to see him, especially his mother who was happy to know that he would be living 'properly' as she termed it, instead of living rough in a tent as though he were a homeless layabout. He spent the few days visiting relatives and of course Malcolm, who was pleased to hear the good news as he had already provided Jack Longstaffe with an excellent reference.

'I would have been most upset if you had not got the job Ted. I gave him a shining reference, only what you deserve, the years of dedication and hard work you have given me. He sounds a nice bloke and said his family are looking forward to you starting. The problem is I will have to look for someone to do your job next winter. Mind you if this doesn't work out you can let me know, and your job will be here for you.'

'It'll work out Malcolm because I'll work damn hard to make sure it does. I have waited far too long for an opportunity like this to let it slip through me fingers. I've met the family a couple of times now and we seem to get along alright. Living away from home especially on campsites has forced me to mix with strangers, so I am not quite the shy lad you knew who left the North East for life in Cumbria. It'll be fine, and the kids seem great. They are both teenagers at grammar school who seem to know what they want out of life. Unfortunately Mrs Longstaffe is in poor health but she's a lovely woman and I know she will make me very welcome. Aye it's new beginnings for me at last. I'd best be off now as I need to buy work clothes before I start, and I reckon I'll get them a lot cheaper over here than in Cumbria.' The two men shook hands, and Malcolm wished him all the best telling him he must never forget it was him who gave him his first job.

'I'll not do that, I will always be grateful to you for what you have taught me and don't think you've seen the last of me either. I'll call in to see you whenever I visit home, though that won't be so regular from now on.' With that he turned and left the car showroom, privately hoping he would never have to work there again. He arrived at the workwear suppliers and took a shopping list from his pocket. He chose two pairs of safety boots, one pair of wellingtons, four work shirts and two pairs of work trousers, one pair of waterproof over trousers, three pullovers, one waterproof jacket, one woollen hat, and one pair of gloves to beat the cold winds. When he was told the price he was pleased that he had always been rather frugal, and did not begrudge spending a relatively large sum of money in order to have the correct clothing needed for his new job. Over the past few years he was used to wearing his old clothes for the casual work he did, and never had any special work gear set aside.

With his shopping bags in the boot of the car, he drove back for one more night with his parents. They had arranged for a couple of family members to join them for a meal as they thought it could be quite some time before they would see him again. Everyone enjoyed the meal, and he thanked them for coming, offering his apologies as he went to bed for an early night as he planned to leave early the next morning.

Around seven the next morning, he drank some tea and ate some toast before putting his last belongings into the car. Once again he said his goodbyes but this time he noticed a tear trickling down his mother's cheek. Not one for showing his affection, he was rather embarrassed and threw her a kiss. Waving goodbye he realised that it could be several months before he saw his mother again and he felt a lump in his throat, then blinked rapidly to hold back the tears, as he felt a tinge of sadness at leaving home.

His drive over from Newcastle to Cumbria via Alston, England's highest market town, was a journey covering an area of exceptional natural beauty, and a route he was familiar with. He would normally pull over at his favourite beauty spots to admire the wonderful scenery but today he wanted to make it back as quickly as possible to arrive at Felix Hill soon after lunch, the time which had been agreed. He chose to make one stop at the florists in Alston where he bought a bouquet of flowers to give to Margaret as a way of expressing his gratitude to her for inviting him to share their home.

As he laid the bouquet on the passenger seat he shook his head and smiled to himself in disbelief. He had never bought any woman, apart from his mother, a bouquet of flowers. 'Well they say there is a first time for everything,' he thought to reassure himself he was doing the right thing.

Spring and autumn were Ted's favourite seasons, and this new start could not have happened at a nicer time of year. He loved to admire the

60

flora and fauna as they began their rebirth thanks to the miracle of nature's renewing cycle. He loved to be able to listen for the first cuckoo and to hear the birds singing from the tree tops and watch them as they collected material to make their nests. The sight of newly born lambs playfully leaping around the fields and the occasional deer made him happy. The anticipation of starting work on a sheep farm at lambing time was almost impossible for him to take in. April was the month to enjoy the longer and warmer days, with only two weeks until Easter, and for Ted that day everything was right with the world.

He arrived around ten o'clock and stopped off in Pooley Bridge at his favourite café. He saw the advert for the job still in the window and suggested to the waitress that it be removed as he was starting work in the next couple of hours. She apologised as she had forgotten but assured him that Mrs Longstaffe had popped in a few days earlier to say the job had been taken. Smiling she peeled the advert from the window and passed it to Ted, 'Would you like to have it as a keepsake?'

He hesitated for a second, then taking it out of her hand, he read it again still unable to believe his luck that he was the successful applicant.

'Will it be your usual Ted, with coffee or tea this morning?'

'Aye the full works thanks, with extra toast to follow. I had an early start this morning travelling over from Northumberland and as I'm very thirsty could you make that a large pot of tea, preferably before breakfast is ready?'

'No problem, breakfast won't take long.' The waitress headed for the kitchen but watched him out of the corner of her eye as he had kept a tight grip on the advert. She saw him put it into his pocket, making sure that it was deep inside as though it were a wad of notes or a valuable cheque he was afraid of losing.

He enjoyed his breakfast and paid his bill handing the waitress a generous tip, as he felt on top of the world. From the café he went to the campsite where he had left most of his belongings and, after dismantling and collecting everything together, he took his worldly possessions and packed them in his car. Jack had told him there was room for his things to be stored at the farm, and he decided it was a good idea to keep them there. He called in to say goodbye and pay his dues with the campsite owners before he took his leave. He thanked them for the wonderful times he had shared with them over the years.

'Remember you are not a stone's throw away from us so make sure you pay us visits whenever you can. Enjoy your new job Ted, and make the most of it as it's the opportunity you have been waiting for.'

'I will and I'll be back to see you again,' he said and set off excited about his future, acknowledging their enthusiastic waves.

The first of April, his start date was a Sunday. As he drove towards the farm the sun appeared from behind the clouds which had begun to lift earlier when he was heading down the steep winding road from Alston. He took this to be a good sign lifting his spirits even higher. He could not remember a time when he felt as happy, since the day he passed his driving test and bought his first car from Malcolm.

The day before his arrival the children had done their usual chores. Muriel and her mother spent some time adding the finishing touches to Ted's bedroom making sure it was comfortable. Michael took Muriel with him on the day of Ted's arrival to make time for Jack and Margaret to welcome him. They showed him his room and the rooms of the house he would share with the family. They appreciated he would need time to himself to settle in and, with the children at school for another week before Easter, he had time with Jack to begin learning the job. He would also get to know Margaret without interruptions from the ever talkative Muriel.

Margaret welcomed him at the door having heard his car coming along the track. As he walked towards her she could see he was carrying a bouquet of flowers over his arm. She felt a warm friendly feeling towards him, as she guessed they would be for her. 'Welcome to our home Ted,' she said in a rather shy tone of voice and offered him her hand.

'These are for you Margaret,' he said, handing the bouquet to her and shaking her hand. He could see she was quite overwhelmed and to save further embarrassment he quickly asked where Jack was.

'He'll be at the kitchen table waiting for you. He's not been in very long from lambing. The ewes are hard at work now delivering their lambs and he has to keep alert to make sure he is there to help any that are in difficulty. Thanks so much for the flowers Ted. I'll go and find a vase to put them in.' She felt slightly self conscious and wondered what

Jack would say considering it was so long since he had bought her any flowers. She pointed Ted in the direction of the kitchen.

'You go straight through and see Jack and I'll be with you shortly.'

'Good to see you Ted and glad you made it on time. Did you have a decent drive across this morning?'

'I certainly did. With today to look forward to I put my foot down pretty hard I can tell you. I made none of my usual stops to admire the views, except for one in Alston where I headed straight to the florists to buy your good lady a bouquet of flowers. Mind you she is the only woman besides my mother I have ever bought flowers for so she is honoured.'

'Putting me to shame you are! I hope you are not going to be spoiling her too much as I can't remember the last time I bought her flowers and she will no doubt remind me of that. All the same I bet she was more than delighted with them.'

'By the expression on her face I believe she was, and she's off looking for a vase to put them in.'

Jack pulled a chair from under the table and beckoned him over. 'Sit yourself down Ted, and let's see where we begin. This is as new to me as it is to you. As you know I've never had anyone working full time for me before and we've never had anyone living in with us but we'll all get used to it. How about we start with a nice cold beer?' He opened the fridge and took out two cans of light ale. 'Bet you are more used to the Newcastle Brown rather than this light stuff.'

'To be honest Jack I am not much of a drinking man. That doesn't mean I don't enjoy a drink but a couple or three is enough for me anytime. I've seen too many drunkards around, and that included my own father on many an occasion.'

'Margaret's not a drinking woman and she doesn't like to see me having too many either, and of course the children are still too young to start the habit. A few evenings a week we may settle down if we have time, and watch some TV or listen to some music with a drop of ale or whatever takes the fancy.'

The door opened just as Jack began pouring the ale into his glass. 'Having an early start today are we?' Margaret said, shocked to see alcohol being drunk so early in the day.

'Just the one, a welcoming drink. Ted has had a tiring morning travelling over but don't worry he tells me he is not a drinker so you will have no problems there. Why not join us, have a tonic or a bitter lemon?'

'No I'm fine I will make myself some tea,' and with a smile on her face she pointed to the flowers and asked, 'so what do you think of these then Jack Longstaffe?'

'I heard about them and I've already warned him he is not to start spoiling you and putting me to shame.'

'I'll take them into the sitting room where it's cooler, that way they will last longer and we'll be able to enjoy their lovely fragrance while we relax in the evenings. That is if we can find the time we are so busy during lambing.'

She returned to the kitchen and sat with the two men for a brief time. Apologising that he must get back to work, Jack asked Ted to make himself at home, and treat the house as he would living with his own parents. He added that he had made a space in a shed for him to keep his outdoor camping gear where it would stay dry until he needed it.

As he headed out Jack said, 'There are more important things outside at the minute, and I'm sure you'll want to get over to see the lambing. It's a busy and tiring time Ted, but I have Dennis and Tom, faithful family friends, who I can always call on to give me a hand whenever I'm in need of extra help, especially since Margaret took ill, and Michael is out and about so much. They are both here today as they knew I needed time with you so you'll meet them soon. Lambing is, as you'll know, a 24 hour job until they are all safely delivered, but Herdwicks are hardy sheep and most of them lamb outside on the in-bye land, and we only take them into the sheds if we think there are problems. About half the ewes have already delivered but there's still a way to go yet. Well I must be off now and will see you when you get yourself sorted out.'

'I understand Jack, you head off and I'll get changed and follow you over just as quick as I can.'

Margaret gave him a tour of the upstairs and showed him his room and where the clean towels were kept and left him to his own devices. He carried his things to his room and sorted the bags containing his new work clothes and changed into them. He looked the part in a dark checked shirt, work trousers and boots - he was ready for the challenge.

Before he left to join Jack he popped his head into the kitchen to let Margaret know he was off.

'Well you certainly look ready for work Ted. Oh and, by the way, will you tell Jack I'll be away to pick the children up within the next half hour or so and I know how excited they will be about seeing you again.'

'Will do,' he replied raising his hand to her at the same time nodding his head in both acknowledgement and disbelief. He went across the yard to find Jack, to meet Dennis and Tom and to mentally 'clock-in' for the start of his exciting new life.

CHAPTER NINE

Ted settled in quickly and Jack reckoned he took to the job like someone who had been born into farming. He never had to be asked twice to do anything, and the family loved Ted as though he were a brother. He was spoken of fondly when introduced to new people and Jack and Margaret refered to him as 'irreplaceable,' 'Jack of all trades and master of none' or 'born to farm this lad.' When said within earshot Ted was embarrassed though secretly proud as he had proved to himself that he was capable of achieving his ambition.

Michael looked up to him as an older brother while Muriel enjoyed teasing him especially about his Geordie accent. She said things like, 'Are yee gannin ta wark with me Da doon the farm the day?' or 'Haad on yee two I'll be wid yee in a couple of shakes of lamb's tail.' Another was 'Are yee picking me and our Michael up fray the school the day?' Her favourite was at evening meals when Margaret wanted to give him a plate of dinner, she turned to her mother and speaking on Ted's behalf, 'Dinna yee be given me ower much tatie there Meggie. Yer ower feedin me I'm getting fat enough wivoot yee giving me huge dollops of everything.' This amused everyone especially Ted as he tried to refrain from using his Geordie, because they struggled to understand what he meant. Of course there were times when he forgot and it was obvious which part of the country he came from. They had many a laugh over it, and he took it all as good fun.

Jack was reaching the point when he knew he could not manage the farm without him or someone just as good. Margaret's health had not improved, and if anything, he worried she was deteriorating quickly. With so much to do to keep everything running smoothly, he would continuously thank Ted knowing how lucky they were to have him working on the farm. This reassured Ted that his job was fairly secure while at the same time he appreciated all that the family had done for him. To

Margaret it was as if she had three children, and she treated him as a son, sometimes having to correct herself forgetting how much older he was than her own children. Ted didn't mind and enjoyed the attention, but for the most part he liked to be with Jack outside on the farm. This arrangement could not have worked out better and they often commented on how pleased they were that Ted had been passing through Pooley Bridge at the time the advert was displayed.

✄ ✄ ✄

The children were growing up quickly and in spite of the obvious difficulties, Jack and Margaret made sure they often had friends around for meals and noticed how they were becoming attracted to the opposite sex. Muriel's Yorkshire friend Katy seemed to be growing up quickly. She came to stay during most of the school holidays. Friends were invited to join them at the farm where they enjoyed listening to music, discussed the latest fashions and did the things teenagers got up to by simply having fun together. However the friendship between the two girls' seemed a little strained as time went on as Katy wanted to spend more time with Michael than she did with Muriel. Whether Michael was as interested in Katy as she appeared to be in him, Muriel was not sure, but she was jealous and concluded Michael was the reason why she had never been invited to Yorkshire. Nearing the end of one of Katy's visits Muriel decided she had to say something and took Michael to one side as though he had committed a crime. In a tone of voice she didn't usually use, Muriel challenged him, 'I know Katy only comes here to see you now Michael, you have to admit it.'

Taken aback Michael replied abruptly, 'For goodness sake Mu what are you talking about? You know I don't have time for girlfriends and besides I don't even fancy her.'

'Well you always seem to be with her, chatting all the time and even when our friends are around she seems to be with you and ignores the rest of us. You don't even seem to bother with many of our other friends either when she's here so don't deny it. You must fancy her so why don't you just admit it?'

Michael's face was a picture. His jaw dropped, his eyes wide from the shock of Muriel's unexpected remarks. He gasped, 'Honestly Mu I only put up with her for your sake. You are always asking her to come here. I can't ignore her when she is living with us even though I try dodging her as much as I can which obviously you have not noticed.'

In retaliation Muriel told him in a slightly raised tone of voice, 'I don't invite her she always asks to come to stay, and now I know why she never asks me to go to visit her in Yorkshire. She wants to come here to see you. She is always talking about boys and says she is allowed to have a boyfriend at home and that her parents don't mind. So that's it. The next time she asks to come to stay I'm going to tell her she can't. I know she won't like it, but I will say that we are all too busy and mother is not well enough these days to have extra guests to look after, which will probably be true anyway, as it's all far too much for her lately.'

'Oh we are being a little madam, and getting into a strop which is not like you, and to be honest sounds rather an unkind thing to do, the number of years she has been visiting us.'

'It probably does sound unkind but she hardly bothers to keep in touch until the school holidays come around and then she immediately asks to come and stay. That tells me that she's only coming to see you and that our friendship means very little to her now.'

'Okay Mu that's up to you, but you must put it across to her in a more decent manner than you are explaining it to me. You have been friends for a lot of years now and it is not like you to be nasty.'

'I won't tell her yet. I'll wait until the next time she rings up to say she wants to come and stay then I will tell her that her last visit left mother very tired and, as she's getting no better, we've decided that it's not possible to have visitors at the moment. That will give her a hint that she may not be invited here again.'

Michael was rather shocked by her attitude and told her firmly, 'I hope you are not turning into a vixen Muriel Longstaffe.' She did not respond so he continued, 'Do you know what, I think you're jealous when she spends time with me and that you don't like it when any girls are hanging around me which isn't very often anyway.'

This brought a swift reaction from her, 'Don't you be daft Michael,' but she knew what he had said was right. She loved knowing that girls found her brother attractive but she did not like to see them getting too close, as she was very possessive. Like any other male of his age he had an eye for a pretty girl, but his training, took up most of his spare time and left him little time for girlfriends. When Muriel saw him with a girl she was always very jealous and intervened whenever she could.

During her time at grammar school, and unbeknown to Michael or so she thought, Muriel had become fond of Scott, a boy in her own year. She tried to make sure that she met him in a crowd so that if Michael was around he wouldn't notice them. She thought he considered her too young for boys, but at a little over fifteen and growing into a shapely young woman she was no different from all the other girls in school. Michael at eighteen was going to finish his education soon, and with his A-levels completed, he planned to put education behind him to concentrate full time on canoeing with Philip. Muriel looked to this as her opportunity to really get to know Scott properly. She did not know that Michael knew all along about her friendship with Scott, but let her carry on thinking he knew nothing. 'Just because we don't have time for girls doesn't mean that Mu can't have fun with the boys,' he told Philip when they spotted them together. It remained their secret until such time as Michael felt it was right to say that he and Philip had known all along.

Muriel was doing her voluntary work at the vets which was one of the highlights of her week, and she was more convinced than ever that this would be her future career. She went in early in the day in order to gain as much experience as possible. If she managed an early lift into Penrith with her mother, father, or Ted she let Scott know that she was having a longer lunch break and they met up. Their friendship grew and, not long after reaching her sixteenth birthday, he was allowed to visit the farm most Sundays where he enjoyed some banter with Jack and Ted, or he went with Muriel to watch Michael and Philip training.

Living and working with the Longstaffe family, and seeing the children having fun, Ted began to feel he had missed out a little on friendships among people his own age. He was invited to join the family whenever there was anyone visiting, young or old, but at times he declined and spent the time alone in his bedroom. The family accepted that there were occasions when he would take time for himself, perhaps to think about his family back in the North East, to read a book or watch television. He had bought a set for his room, and they never questioned any of his decisions or pestered him to change his mind.

'Feeling a bit tired,' he said rather than offend by saying he would prefer to be alone. The truth was that he no longer liked being alone but, admiring Muriel's beauty, not only in her personality but also how shapely and mature she had become, he found it difficult to hide his feelings for her. He had never felt like this about a woman before and found it easier not to be to close to her. Although he knew it was wrong, he watched her with Scott and wished it was him holding her hand or strolling arms around each other, as they wandered around the farmyard laughing and joking. It was too painful to watch when he saw them kissing passionately when they thought no-one was looking, but try as he might it was hard to resist watching her. His feelings made him feel guilty. 'Why have I never felt this way before? After all Muriel has done nothing to encourage me in any way, and she is very young.'

He lay alone at night and, looked back over his life, remembering how much he enjoyed his own company as a child, and how earning money to achieve his goal became his priority. He concluded that moving around from place to place all the time must have been the reason he didn't become interested in girls. He thought, 'I was never in the same place long enough for women to become interested in me or me in them. Now that I'm living here I've realised what a wonderful thing marriage and family life would be.' Satisfied in his own mind about the reasons for being single for so long, he reckoned the feelings he had for Muriel were perfectly natural, and would have happened before now with some other girl if he had led a less nomadic life.

'At 27 I'm too old for her anyway,' he convinced himself, but that did not stop him admiring her. He tried his best to think about something else knowing that, it was unthinkable for anything to happen between them. He thought, 'How would everyone feel if they knew? After all Jack and Margaret treat me like a son, Michael and Muriel like their brother. It seems I'm too close to them.' He was riddled with guilt, but nothing stopped his feelings for her. 'If ever Jack and Margaret found out about my feelings for their daughter I am sure they would sack me on the spot,' he thought. The terrible thought of losing the job he loved so much, but worse than that, never seeing Muriel again passed through his mind every day and, with his heart aching he continued to admire her in secret.

His feelings were made no easier as Margaret seldom drove the children around due to her health and, as Jack preferred to work on the farm, more often than not they asked Ted to help. When he was alone in the car with her it was difficult, but he never made her aware of his feelings and continued to hide his feelings well. Selfishly he hoped that one day her romance with Scott would end then, perhaps as she concentrated more on her career she would see him as an attractive man rather than the Geordie lad she teased and looked to as an older brother. His hopes were never high and he often despaired. By then he had lived with the family for over two years and had never talked about girls and never brought a girl to the farm. He was confident the family would never discover his secret assuming, as his own family had done, that he preferred the single life and would remain a bachelor. Muriel was now sixteen, eleven years younger than Ted, and no-one guessed his true feelings.

CHAPTER TEN

Michael spent most of his days across the lake training with Philip under Geoff's watchful eye and as a result of their dedication and hard work they went from strength to strength. Since he had finished school daily instruction sessions from Geoff increased. Geoff continued to have unquestionable faith in their future success and that, one day, they would compete in the Olympic games. They were unable to qualify for the 1980 Moscow Olympics, but Geoff was determined that they would make it to the Los Angeles Olympics in 1984. They needed to work extremely hard and find sponsors to help them raise the money to get there, but Geoff had no doubts that they would achieve it. All three were dedicated to the sport and determined to bring pride to their families and to Cumbria.

Back at the farm Michael shouted upstairs to his mother who was having an afternoon rest that he was home.

'Okay Michael I'll be down soon.' His mother's voice was so weak he could barely hear what she said, so he ran up the stairs two at a time to make sure she was alright. Popping his head around the bedroom door he assured her, 'There's no need to rush up. I'm going over to see if Dad needs an extra pair of hands tonight and if he doesn't, I'll be off again to the lake for some leisurely practice. I don't want to miss the opportunity on a night like this if I know they can manage without me. You stay where you are for now and I'll be back to let you know what I'm doing.' Leaving her to rest he set off to find his father when he saw Ted returning with Muriel. The school run was one of Ted's regular jobs. He didn't mind the task but he was certain it would never be allowed if Muriel's parents knew about his feelings for their daughter. Pleased to see them, Michael waved then continued to find his father who was busy in the hay barn.

'Hello Dad, everything okay?'

'Fine son have you had a good day?'

'Great, though very hot and tiring at times but we managed a few hours. I was wondering if you will be needing any help from me tonight?' Michael was always willing to help but knew that his father would only take up his offer if he was really busy as Ted was always willing to work whenever necessary.

'No not tonight son, Ted will be back just now and we can manage all that needs to be done here for the rest of today. Are you planning to go to the lake again as it's such a lovely night?'

'Yes, if you are sure you don't need me. Ted's already back with Mu so if everyone is happy about it then I wouldn't mind going out again, as I need to keep in peek condition with all the extra competitions we are entering over the next few months. It's a perfect night and it will begin to cool down a bit soon which will make it ideal.'

Jack knew his son was totally committed to what he was doing, and he could not refuse him the time he needed for training in order to fulfil his ambition. Even though he would love to spend more time with Michael he knew he could never hold him back.

'Off you go then, but check everything is alright with your mother and that Muriel can manage everything that needs to be done before you go.' Then as always his warning words to him, 'Take care and watch what you are doing out there.'

'I will Dad I'm fine,' he acknowledged in his usual confident voice as though to say, 'Stop worrying nothing's going to happen.'

As he crossed back to the house he met Ted who never wasted a moment and went straight back out to work.

'It's been a lovely day Michael. Bet you and Philip have had a good session today but tiring in weather like this.'

'We did, it was a bit too hot and Geoff worked us extra hard but only as needs must if we are going to succeed.' He felt slightly guilty about going out again, but Ted was now so much a part of the family he was as determined as everyone else to see Michael succeed. In a quieter voice he said, 'Dad says you won't need me tonight so I'm off to have a sandwich, and then I'm going down to the lake for a couple of hours whilst the weather's so nice. Do you know what Mu is up to tonight?'

'I believe she's revising for an exam she has in the morning so I don't think we'll see much of her tonight. Enjoy yourself and take care.'

'Alright, I'll catch up with her over a sandwich and then I'll be off, see you later Ted.' The two continued in opposite directions.

Muriel was busy making herself a sandwich when she heard Michael coming into the kitchen. 'Hi there you okay?'

'Yes and you?' then without waiting for her reply he began to sweet-talk her. 'Who has the best sister in the world who just loves to make her favourite brother sandwiches so he can go back out again for a couple of hours.'

'Now there's something different I must say,' she said smiling at him. She made him some sandwiches and poured them each a glass of milk. Sitting together at the table they caught up on the day's events, always interested to know what the other one had been doing. Before he left he made sure she was happy with the arrangements for the rest of the day and that everything was fine.

'You're sure you won't need any help from me tonight? How did you think mother was when you came in from school?' Michael was concerned their mother was having to take more rest than usual, and was aware that they talked less about her worsening condition, possibly as they feared that she wasn't going to get any better.

'She's fine and says she'll be getting up later to cook the dinner as she knows I need time at the moment to revise for my exams. It's not a problem for you to go off for a while you know that, and don't worry about us. If she struggles there are three of us here to help her. Michael you know how much it will mean to see you and Philip at the next Olympics standing on the podium proudly displaying your medals.'

'I know, so let's hope we don't let any of you down then, but we all know the competition is extremely tough at Olympic level so it will not be easy.' After pausing for a moment's thought he moved towards her and putting his hands on her shoulders he pulled her close to him, and gave her a hug. He said, 'You're a good lass Mu. I couldn't be doing this if you were not willing, like father and Ted, to take over some of the things I could be doing at home. I don't know what I would do without you. In fact I don't know what any of us would do without you.' He gave her a peck on the cheek, turned and raced up the stairs to tell his mother, where he was going. Poking his head around her bedroom door he said, 'Nobody seems to mind me going out again, so if you're feeling better Mam, I'll be on my way.'

'No problem Michael I'm feeling a lot better thanks. I just think this hot weather can be a bit too much for me. That's why I need to rest during the day. It helps restore some energy so I am able to cook dinner which you so much deserve, you all work so hard.' Sitting up she was able to see him better and continued, 'Muriel has a lot on with exams at the moment so I don't like asking too much of her. I'll make the dinner a little later which saves me having to rush, and if you're not back when it's ready I'll keep yours hot for you. Off you go then, be careful and don't forget to keep an eye on the time. It's getting later and later when you arrive home and we all start to worry when you're out there on your own.'

Giving her a wink and a cheerful smile he assured her he would be fine. 'I'll be off then - see you at dinner.' At the bottom of the stairs he grabbed two sets of keys, one for the old boathouse and the other for the moped his father had bought him, to save transporting him around every day. He kick started the engine and was off down the farm track eager to get back on the lake.

'That son of ours never seems to rest and he is growing up so fast I can't keep up with him,' thought Margaret, having watched him turn swiftly from the bedroom and take off down the stairs. 'Those two boys are going to do us parents proud one day that's for sure. I just hope I'm around long enough to see it.' Then, ignoring the nauseating fear the thought had brought, she dragged herself slowly from her bed reminding herself, 'It's a long time until the next Olympics and with my condition those doctors are certainly going to have to work a miracle if I'm to be around to watch them succeed. One thing is certain, I must never let Muriel or the boys know how ill I am.'

Her hand wiped away a tear that was trickling down her cheek, and she tried to brush the thoughts to one side. After struggling to dress she went to the bathroom to tidy herself up before going downstairs.

'Is that you up and about Mam?' Muriel shouted upstairs.

'Yes I won't be long I'm just brushing my hair.'

Muriel cleared away the plates and glasses she and Michael had used, and boiled the kettle to make her mother a cup of tea knowing that was the first thing she wanted when she came downstairs.

'Tea will be ready in a minute,' Muriel said looking slightly shocked to see that her mother still had that 'just out of bed' appearance and seemed to be very weary. Watching her as she slowly crossed the kitchen and slumped onto the chair, she looked as though she had just finished a hard day's work, rather than having had a long afternoon's rest. She pretended not to notice how weak she appeared and asked, 'Would you like something to eat with your tea Mam?'

'No thanks I had lunch with your father and Ted, so a nice cup of tea will do me for now. Have you had a good day at school, and how is Scott today?'

'Not bad, everyone is worrying about the exams of course. I didn't see much of Scott as we both needed to revise during the lunch break, and I must do some more tonight for my maths exam tomorrow, so if there's anything you need me to do I must get on with it as soon as possible. I take it you were awake and Michael told you he'd gone to the lake?'

'Yes he told me his plans and came and said bye. I worry though that since he finished school he might be doing far too much. He has been with Philip and Geoff nearly all day and now he's away again, practice, practice, and more practice. He must surely get tired at times!'

'He's alright Mam, he's as fit as a fiddle and you know what this means to him. If he was tired he wouldn't go out again at night. We know how intense this training is going to be for them and that they must keep it up to keep up their strength and remain focused. You know he loves what he does and would rather be doing this at the moment than anything else in his world. Knowing father has Ted to help him and me to help you he can do it no problem.'

She crossed the room to give her mother a kiss on the forehead and rebuked her in a jovial tone. 'Will you stop worrying about him Mrs Longstaffe. You know it can't be doing your health any good. Now is there anything you want me to do before I start my revision?'

'I know you're right Muriel. He's best doing something he loves and there's plenty of time for him to do other things later in life. Now then, there's nothing urgent needs doing here and I can manage as I'm only cooking the meal for tonight which I've already told Michael will be a little later than usual. Now why don't you go outside to revise and enjoy the sun and some fresh air?'

'I was going to anyway so will see you later, but I'll come and help you with the dinner.' She picked up her school books and headed off outside to a sunny spot for some serious revision.

✄ ✄ ✄

Leaving the farm track, Michael found the road busy which didn't surprise him on such a beautiful evening. Walkers were out in large numbers looking rather hot and tired from the intense heat, and probably exhausted having been up on the fells most of the day. The cars were slow as the volume of traffic was heavier than usual on the narrow road. He raced along as fast as he could and dodged between walkers and stationary cars which had pulled over to let traffic going in the opposite direction pass. When he reached Howtown Pier, he saw several passengers boarding the steamer which would take them over to the other side of the lake where many of them would stay overnight. School children who had kayaked under the supervision of instructors from the Howtown Centre were busy tying everything up for the night and, like the walkers, they looked rather exhausted.

A short distance along the road Michael arrived at the boathouse and, after unlocking the door, he removed his kayak and paddle. He left the door partially open as he changed into his wetsuit and helmet. Once the moped was inside he locked the door and, carried his kayak and paddle, to the shore just a few minutes walk away. The lake was still busy with sailing boat and kayak lovers making the most of the glorious spring evening. By the time he was ready to paddle off, the Ullswater Steamer had left the pier and was steadily making its way through the water. Comfortably positioned, he set off, this time for a relaxing hour without the demands of training with Philip and Geoff. Calling this his 'leisure time' he took things easily, relaxing to let the pressures of life pass over him. He listened to the gentle sound of the water lapping against the kayak as he paddled towards the centre of the lake. The cool breeze swept across his sunburned face and he reminded himself how lucky he was to take part in such a wonderful sport.

He was grateful to his parents and thought to himself, 'Considering Mam and Dad are not the wealthiest of farmers they have been very generous allowing me the opportunity to do this. Employing Ted when they can ill afford it - they must have great faith in me. One thing for sure I must not let any of them down, Mam, Dad, Mu, and even Ted, they have given up so much for me in their different ways. I only wish Mam was well again, then Mu would not be missing out on so many things. She's so unselfish. I know she would never have it any other way, and that's why I love her.'

Paddling leisurely across the lake deep in thought he continued to dwell on how lucky he was to have so many people willing to give up so much for him. 'Get moving a bit faster Michael Longstaffe you have to prove to everyone in 1984 that it has all been worthwhile.' Realising how quickly the time was passing, he increased his speed and concentrated on his technique, aware that by the time he returned to the shore the sun would be setting in what was turning into a beautiful red sky. The spectacular colours reflected on the calm water made an overwhelming scene of absolute beauty. The sunset brought to an end what had been for him another wonderful day as one of the country's Olympic hopefuls.

CHAPTER ELEVEN

It was 8.40pm and the men were enjoying a cold beer while Muriel was putting the finishing touches to the dinner table, putting a small bowl of flowers in the centre, and her favourite prawn cocktail starter on the table. The aroma from Margaret's steak pie, in rich brown gravy with onions, topped with delicious pastry was tantalising their taste buds. There were also mashed potatoes, cabbage and carrots. They were hungry but were waiting for Michael who they expected at any moment.

'I hope he's not going to be much longer as I like us all to eat together,' said Margaret already worried. She ignored Muriel's earlier request to stop fretting. 'He doesn't realise the time when he gets out on the lake - he gets carried away in his own thoughts that's the problem, and he forgets how soon it will be dark.' Her voice sounded anxious as she added, 'we'll wait a little while longer before we begin as he's sure to be home any time now.'

'He shouldn't be much longer Margaret, and you can't blame him for making the most of such a lovely evening. We'll hang on until about nine and if he's not back then we'll start without him.' Jack turned to Ted, 'I bet you're hungry too.'

'Me too,' Muriel joined in. 'If he doesn't hurry up I think I'll pass out from heat as well as hunger.' She turned on the tap and let the water run for a while to make sure it was as cold as possible to drink. 'Anyone else want water before I turn it off?'

'Think I can manage another beer what about you Ted?'

'Sounds a good idea to me. How about you Margaret can we tempt you with anything?'

'Not at the moment thanks,' she said. Eating and drinking was the last thing she wanted when her thoughts focused entirely on listening for Michael's moped speeding back up the track.

'I'll start mashing the potatoes and serving the vegetables. It will be nearly 9 o'clock by then and he's sure to be back.'

'Good idea Muriel. It's a shame to spoil the dinner by.' As she reached for the milk and butter from the fridge, Margaret swayed slightly and had to grab hold of a chair back.

'Steady on there Marg,' Jack cut short her name as he quickly reacted and reached across to save her from falling. 'What's that all about, you secretly been on the beer?'

Not amused Margaret didn't reply but brushed herself down and returned to the fridge. Then she made a swift exit from the kitchen.

'Do you think Mam's alright Dad?' Muriel asked as she had never seen her mother so unsteady on her feet and was very concerned.

'It's probably just the heat. It's very hot in here tonight. Don't worry I'll follow her in a minute and make sure she's alright.'

Muriel mashed the potatoes and served out the vegetables. Worried about her mother, she didn't have her usual banter with Ted. Jack had gone to check on Margaret while Muriel put the plates in the oven and turned the temperature low.

'Your mother will be fine,' Ted reassured Muriel in a not very convincing tone. 'She just worries far too much about everything as you know, but we are all here for her, and Michael will no doubt be home any minute as he's never very late.'

'He is later than usual tonight though Ted, you must admit that.'

'Yes but there will be a good reason for it. There are lots of people out and about on a lovely night like this and he might just be involved in conversation with someone.'

Jack and Margaret returned to the kitchen. Jack looked relieved but Margaret looked worried which made her look older than her years.

'It's turned nine now Mam. Don't you think we should begin?'

'Yes we will dear. You must all be starving as it's getting very late.'

Pulling out a chair for her mother Muriel sat next to Ted, who commented on how appetising the starter looked. 'Can't wait to try this - it's my favourite.'

No-one wanted to talk much and Ted, aware that the family were so close to Michael, understood why they were now very concerned about him. He tried not to show his own feelings and promised, 'If he's not back by the time we have eaten I'll go out and start looking for him and

I bet we meet on the road somewhere nearby.' The silence continued and he decided he had best say nothing further for fear of upsetting anyone. First course finished Muriel tidied the table and picked up the oven cloth to lift the hot plates to the table, along with the golden crusted steak pie.

'I can't wait to get my knife and fork into that pie - it looks delicious,' said Jack trying to lift the mood, but had no response from his wife.

Margaret picked up a knife and a large serving spoon, cut the pie and dished out a generous portion. She made sure there was enough left for Michael, and put the pie back into the oven with his plate, turning the dial down even lower.

'Would you like a drink with your meal?' asked Muriel wondering what might be going through her mother's mind.

'Yes please just water, as cold as you can get it, which reminds me I need to be making more ice cubes with the weather as hot as this.'

'I'll make some later on. It'll be cold enough for you if I leave the tap running for a while.'

Jack, tried to appear calm and attempted to take everyone's attention away from Michael by discussing the meal.

'I would never have thought you could improve on that pie Margaret, but you'll agree with me Ted it is exceptional tonight?'

'It most certainly is, and I bet you agree as well Muriel.'

'I do - she's a great cook my mother and she teaches me well, but I know I will never make as good a cook as you will I Mam?'

'With practice you will. You're already showing signs of being able to put a good meal on the table, and as simple healthy cooking is quite easy you won't fail to keep a family fed.'

Ted's imagination wandered as he thought how wonderful it would be if Muriel at some time in the future cooked for him as his wife. Then quickly guilt set in and he felt ashamed of himself. 'Ted Thornton how could you even think about such a thing at a time like this, when everyone is so concerned about Michael and you are turning your thoughts to Muriel.' He looked at the clock - it was now past 9.30pm and, it was obvious the tension around the table was increasing.

'Do you fancy another beer Ted?' Jack asked thinking this might help to relax them.

'No thanks Jack, best I give it a miss. If I have to go looking for

Michael just now I need to have my wits about me.'

'Aye you're right there lad, it was wrong of me to suggest it.'

'I think you'd best give it a miss as well Jack, you know I don't like you having too many beers. It's not good for you and I think you need to be sober until Michael is home safe.'

He realised Michael was the reason Margaret did not want him to have another beer but he smiled to himself thinking, 'If only she realised how little alcohol there is in two small bottles of light ale.' He agreed and suggested that a coffee might be a good idea, and Muriel left the table to make it for him.

'Any more for any more?' she asked as she put the kettle on to boil.

It was almost ten and still no Michael. The expressions on their faces, the rubbing together of hands and the lack of conversation, made it clear real anxiety was now setting in.

'Would you like me to go looking for him Jack?' Ted asked, remembering his promise. He realised that the family were convinced something might have happened.

Muriel jumped in saying, 'I'll go with you Ted.'

Her father decided this was not a good idea, 'I think it would be better if you stay with your mother. I'll go with Ted as it's dark now so it will be better if us two go.'

'Alright Dad I'll stay and look after Mam, maybe I will manage somehow to take her mind off things for a while.' She knew there was little chance of this and, as expected Margaret made no comment, her expression spoke for her.

The men grabbed their jackets in case the night air suddenly turned cooler. Jack took the car keys and a spare set of keys to the boathouse. Ted suggested he drove. They both knew the road like the back of their hands but as Jack was so worried about his son, common sense told him that it would be safer for Ted to drive.

Ted drove steadily around the narrow twisting bends leading down to the road, headlights on full, their eyes focused straight ahead, they both silently prayed for the single headlight from Michael's moped to appear along the road. Without mentioning a word to Jack, Ted secretly glanced from one side of the road to the other for fear Michael had had an accident and was lying somewhere in the roadside. Few words were spoken but Ted felt he needed to break the silence and tried to reassure Jack.

'Michael's a sensible lad he won't have done anything stupid. He will, just as Margaret said earlier, have got carried away in his own world and not realised the time.'

'I hope you're right Ted but I have a gut feeling something has happened. Call it parental instinct if you like, but I'm really worried as it is so unlike him to be this late.'

Unable to comfort him, he increased his speed slightly and said, 'We'll be at the boathouse in about five minutes and I bet we find him happily locking up and about to head for home.'

'I pray to God you're right Ted,' Jack's voice was weak and shaking at the very thought of finding anything other than that.

Pulling onto the grass verge alongside the boathouse Ted switched the engine off, and in the stillness of the night they listened for the familiar sounds of Michael locking up and starting the moped. Taking torches from the glove box Ted locked the car, still listening, but the only sound was the gentle lapping of the water on the shoreline. Shining their torches to light the way they headed for the boatshed and were shocked to find it still locked. Ted took the keys from his pocket and said that he would check inside, thinking he would spare Jack the shock if he found the moped and not the kayak. His hand trembled as he turned the key afraid of what he would find. He drew in a deep breath, pulled the door ajar and shone the torch inside. As he feared the moped was still in the place where he had hoped the kayak would be. In the darkness Jack could not see Ted's stunned expression before he broke the news to him.

'It's not good Jack,' he paused to control his own emotions before he could bring himself to continue. 'There's only the moped in there Jack so he must still be out there somewhere.'

Jack cried out in disbelief, 'Oh my God no... he would never stay out on the lake in the dark.' His knees gave way and he collapsed to the ground.

Ted sat beside him and put his arm tight around his shoulder where he felt and heard Jack's racing heartbeat pounding through his body. Knowing he must stay calm, he suggested they search the shoreline together for a few yards in each direction. After going as far as they could and not finding anything they returned to the car to consider the best action to take.

Jack sobbed uncontrollably. Ted found this hard to cope with but knew he must take care and, despite his own feelings, he had to keep positive for Jack's sake.

'We must get to a telephone as quickly as possible Jack. I'll drive us along to the Lakes Edge and ring for help from there.'

Jack couldn't bring himself to answer. They made there way to the hotel and Jack tried to gather his thoughts in order to help Ted organise a search. Arriving at Lakes Edge they went to reception where the night-shift receptionist, who knew the family, was sitting at her desk. By the look on their faces she knew instantly something was wrong.

Ted asked, 'Can we use the phone? Michael's gone missing, his kayak's not in the boathouse and we need to ring for help urgently.'

'Of course you can,' she said as she passed the phone to him.

He dialled 999 and explained to the emergency call centre telephonist, 'We need the Police and Lake Rescue. A family member is missing on the lake. He went out early evening in his kayak and has not returned.'

'Where are you ringing from?'

'The Lakes Edge Hotel at Ullswater, he stores his kayak just along the road from here near Howtown. We have checked and he's not been back and it's far later than he would ever stay out.'

'Stay at the hotel. We'll get onto the Outward Bound Lake Rescue and will be back in touch with you as quickly as possible.'

'Thanks, thanks again,' then he passed the phone back to the receptionist who knew Michael well. Badly shaken by the news, she tried to be professional and remain calm.

'We're full up tonight, but if you would like to wait in the staff room away from passing guests, I can arrange for someone to fetch you a pot of tea. I'll double check with Brian, the duty manager tonight, but I know he will be pleased to help and won't mind at all.'

The manager was only too willing to oblige and said he would take them to the staff room.

'We have got to let Margaret and Muriel know they will be worried sick by now,' Jack's voice trembled with fear at the thought of having to pass on this terrible news.

'Leave that for the time being Jack, besides I don't think we are the right ones to be telling them anyway. I suggest the police are the best people to do that while we wait here to find out what we should do next.'

Brian appeared and shook hands with the two men and offered kind words before leading them to the staff room where a waitress brought in a tray of hot drinks and some brandy.

Brian explained, 'I've already given instructions that no member of staff is to enter the staff room until further notice, and that they can use the kitchen tonight when they are due a break from duty.'

Ted thanked him and watched him leave the room before he sat down and wondered what the rest of the night would bring. He poured them each a coffee and brandy, and thought about what they should do for the next few hours.

He said, 'You've got to take a rest. You've had an awful shock. You need to get that drink down you as it's going to be a very long night. All we can do is sit here for the time being and leave everything to the police and lake rescue. It won't be easy, but we have no choice, there isn't anything we can do until daybreak. It's best left to the experts who will be searching through the night.'

In a silent prayer he asked God, 'Please let them find him safe and well.' As they tried to stretch out and settle down he remembered that they would soon be interrupted by a visit from the police who would need as much information as they could give them.

CHAPTER TWELVE

The sound of an unfamiliar car coming up the farm track alerted the waiting pair. 'That's not Dad's car,' Muriel said in a panicked voice looking across to her mother. She jumped out of her chair and anxiously waited the knock on the door.

'I'll answer it,' Margaret offered but dreaded who she would find at the other side.

Muriel said, 'We'll answer it together. It could be anyone at this time of the night.'

The officer knew they were still up waiting for news from the lights on in the downstairs rooms. He knocked firmly at the door.

'Mrs Longstaffe?

Making out in the darkness the police uniform she yelled, 'Oh my God what's happened?' She lifted both arms towards her chest as though to save her heart from failing.

'I think it would be best if I come inside?'

'Of course officer forgive me.' Stepping aside she let Muriel show him into the kitchen.

'What's happened to Michael? I know it's Michael. Something's happened hasn't it?' Muriel pleaded for information in a state near to hysterics.

'We don't know yet. So let's sit down and then I will give you all the information I have up to now.'

He looked sympathetically at them and assured Muriel that all they definitely knew was that Michael had not returned his kayak to the boatshed. There was no further news on what had happened.

'So what's happening now? Where are Jack and Ted, and what are they doing now?' Margaret desperate for answers wanted to know everything as soon as possible.

'They are at the Lakes Edge Hotel where they made their emergency call. They found the boathouse locked with Michael's moped still inside and after a search of the shoreline they found nothing, so they rang us from the hotel and we arranged for Lake Rescue to go out and begin a search straight away. Meanwhile several officers are combing a large area of the shoreline where he might be expected to come ashore. A couple of our officers are at the hotel now gathering as much information as possible, and they will suggest they stay there until daybreak when they can join in the search. Is it possible that Michael may have met someone he knows and is sitting quietly along the shoreline chatting away quite unaware of the worry it could cause? It has been known to happen before when we have been called out, especially when the weather is as hot as it has been today.'

'I assure you officer this wouldn't be the case with Michael. You see he is one of the two boys you may have heard about who are training for the Olympics and they are always home early to be sure that they have a good night's rest in order to be up early next morning for training. You see they train every day.'

'Where do they do their training? Is it at this side of the lake?'

'No, they train about two miles this side of Glenridding with Geoff their instructor who has the Canoeing Club over there.' Then stopping for breath and lowering her head, through sheer exhaustion, she continued. 'Michael had already been over there all day with Philip his co-partner when he decided, as it was such a nice night, he would have a couple of hours out on his own which he often does.'

'What are the chances that he may have decided to paddle over to the club again tonight and is still there now?'

Muriel decided to take over as she could see her mother was desperately concerned. She feared something might happen to her as her breathing was becoming more rapid and shallow.

'Michael never paddles over to Geoff's. It's too far away. He likes to call nights like tonight his 'leisure time' away from serious training where he enjoys plodding along at his own pace and in his own kayak. I know for certain that he won't have done anything like that.'

'Okay lass I understand how hard this is for you both, but I assure you everyone will be doing everything they can and will not give up until they find him. As there is little either of you can do until morning I think

I'll take my leave and suggest you try and get some rest. Myself or a colleague will be in touch the minute we have news. Now, before I go are you sure you'll be alright until then?'

'Well I'm very worried about my mother. You see she has a bad heart and, this is not helping.'

'Would you like me to send an officer to come over and spend the rest of the night with you?'

'What do you think Mam, will you be okay?'

'I think we'll be alright thanks. We'll try and get some sleep knowing Jack and Ted will not be back before morning.'

'If you're absolutely sure then I'll make my way back and see what's happening, but should you need anything urgently don't hesitate to ring and assistance will be here as quickly as possible. I realise it will be hard for you to sleep but it would be best for you both if you can manage a couple of hours. I'll be stopping off at the hotel to let your husband know I have visited and to tell him how you both are. Now if you'll excuse me I'll head off.'

Muriel saw him out asking him again to let them know immediately they heard something.

'I'll do that, now you look after your mother and try to get her up to her bed for a sleep.'

'I will. Goodnight officer.'

'Goodnight Muriel.'

❧ ❧ ❧

The area around the boathouse and hotel was packed with police cars and officers with torches searching the shoreline. Outward Bound Rescue were out on the water, and in the hotel staff room two officers were interviewing Jack and Ted.

'Does your son normally stay out this late on the lake?'

'Never, he's always home around nine at the latest and that is why we came looking for him as we knew something must have happened to him.'

'I can vouch for that officer. I work at the farm and live with the family and as Jack says, he's never home more than a few minutes after nine even on these lighter nights.'

'You say he trains with the Glenridding Canoe Club and that their son pairs with him. That being the case I think we should give them a ring and ask if they have seen or heard from him tonight.'

'I would doubt that very much, as he's already been with them all day. I'd rather we waited until morning before you contact them as I know how distraught they will be on hearing the news.'

Ted agreed with Jack and the police officer decided they should wait another couple of hours before going to Glenridding. 'We don't want to be alarming too many people as word will get around fast enough.'

The officer who had visited the farm tapped on the staff room door and came in. 'How are you Jack?'

'Bearing up but only just.'

'I've been to see your wife and daughter and informed them of all that is happening. They are obviously deeply distressed, but your daughter said she will try to get her mother to take a rest for a couple of hours. I doubt if they will manage it but I've told them if they need anything at all to get in touch immediately. I offered to send an officer along to sit with them but they said they would be alright.'

'I'd like to ring and speak to them as soon as possible,' Jack said. He felt desperate to hear their voices.

'I told them I would be calling in to see you to let you know how they are, so I think it would be better if you left it for a while longer as they might just be lucky enough to catch a couple of hours sleep which they need. Your daughter did seem very worried about your wife, who I understand has a bad heart,'

'She is very ill officer and I think it is a lot of responsibility for Muriel to have to deal with on her own. I think it would be better if you send someone along to be with them as soon as you can?'

'If that's what you want by all means I'll arrange for someone to be with them in a couple of hours.'

Ted, torn between the three of them, wished he could be in both places at once but knew this was impossible and he needed to support Jack. His thoughts though were with Margaret and Muriel alone at the farm not knowing what was happening. 'They must be worried sick by now and I can imagine how they are both feeling,' he thought. How much he yearned to be able to go and comfort them, to put his arms around them both to assure them that everything possible was being done to find their beloved son and brother. His thoughts were interrupted by Jack's slightly raised voice.

'Michael would never take risks. He is expert in his sport, trained to the highest standard by Geoff. That's why we never worry when he is on the lake alone. He can roll a kayak several times in succession. They have had to become experts at survival in both the two man and one man kayaks.'

The officer continued, 'I'm sorry I have to ask this, but I take it he would be wearing a life-jacket?'

Ted stepped in quickly as he could see that Jack was agitated by the questions.

'He was, I would have seen it hanging in the boatshed if he wasn't and, besides, he would never go out without wearing one, would he Jack? He's too professional for that.'

'No never, and he always checks to make sure his gear is up to standard.' Putting his head in his hands Jack knew that Michael would never short cut safety for pleasure. This was why it was difficult for him to believe that something could have happened.

The interview over, the officer suggested that they have something to eat before joining in the search at daybreak.

'I'll ring reception to order us some tea and toast. He's right Jack we need to eat something and as dawn is about to break by the time we have eaten, we'll be able to go out and see how things are going for ourselves.'

☙ ☙ ☙

When they left the hotel, reality hit them. There were people everywhere who had come to help with the search. Guests and staff from the hotel were out helping, as news had spread around the area. Rescue boats from Howtown, and the nearby Sailing Club had joined in, and tourist and campers were helping. Jack stunned by the number of willing helpers turned sharply when he recognised the voice speaking to him from behind.

'They've got to find him Jack. Whatever would we do without him?'

'Geoff, oh my God,' then seeing Philip close by, 'you've both heard then?'

'Yes, the police rang us about an hour ago so we came straight over.' Jack could tell by the look on Philip's face that it was almost too much for him to bear. Ted put his arm around his shoulder and tried to console him. 'I understand Philip, it's almost too much for you to take in but we have to believe he'll be alright until such time as we are told anything different.'

'It can't happen Ted. He's my best mate and is such an expert at kayaking. It's impossible for something to happen to him he could roll a kayak so many times and always come out of it safely. It's too much to even think about.' As tears appeared he pushed Ted's arm from around his shoulder and headed off to a quiet area to deal with the shock in his own way.

The search continued for a further two hours then two grim faced officers headed towards Jack. They took him to one side leading him by the arm. Trembling, he knew what was to come.

'They've found him Jack. It's bad news. Let's get you somewhere comfortable.' Jack asked for Ted to join them and while one of the officers went to fetch him, the other remained silent helping Jack to one of the police cars, where they waited for Ted before they told them where and how he was found.

'They found him slumped in his kayak drifting near the edge of lake. His paddle is missing and it appears he must have taken ill. It seems the only logical reason at the moment, and until a full enquiry is carried out, we won't know exactly what happened.'

Jack was barely able to ask where his son was.

'Your son will have to be taken to the mortuary where someone will need to come to identify the body.'

Through his tears Jack looked across to Ted who had already read his thoughts.

'Could you do that for me?' but before Ted answered the officer said, 'This doesn't need to be done right now. Some time later will be fine as it will take a while for them to take him across. I think it would be better if you went home to your family. I'll take you both in the police car while a colleague drives your vehicle home for you.'

Ted handed the car keys to him. They both dreaded the moment they arrived home to tell Margaret and Muriel the devastating news. They feared the effect this would have on Margaret, and couldn't begin to imagine how Muriel would accept her brother would be gone forever.

❧ ❧ ❧

The events that followed the most shocking day of their lives moved quickly. Ted was their rock, identifying Michael's body when Jack and Margaret were too distraught to visit the mortuary. The family doctor was called to increase Margaret's medication. Ted dealt with many of the necessary calls including the one to the school's headteacher who was deeply shocked on hearing the news.

The headteacher, Neil Fletcher, sent a message to the family via Ted. 'Word had already reached school that someone, possibly Michael was missing on the lake but no-one knew for certain it was him. It's very distressing news for everyone. Michael was one of our most popular boys and there will be lots of pupils who will find this hard to come to terms with. Our hearts go out to Muriel and the family, please pass on our sincere condolences on behalf of the entire school.' Mr. Fletcher was full of compassion for the family, and understood that Muriel would not be able to take her exams, and offered to help in whatever way he could.

'I'll pass your message on Mr Fletcher and someone will be in touch regarding Muriel at some later date.' He put the receiver down and wondered how Muriel would ever be able to face going back to school to continue her studies.

A day or two later, gathered around the kitchen table, the place for most family discussions, Margaret put forward her personal wish. 'I know this may sound very morbid to you all but I would like us to buy a family plot in St. Peter's churchyard. I want us all to be together again when the inevitable time comes when we have to leave this world. I don't even want it to be debated as it's something I've thought very seriously about. I feel very strongly about it so I hope you agree.'

'If that's what you want Margaret I'm sure Muriel and I will be happy to see it through. I'll deal with it, though we all need to visit the churchyard to choose the plot.'

Muriel could not comment. It was almost impossible for her to comprehend that a day would come when all her family would be buried in a graveyard.

'Are you okay Muriel? I know this is hard for you to have to think about but it has to be done.' Jack was concerned as he watched his daughter's complexion turn to a paler shade of white.

'I understand what you're asking, and don't worry, I'll be alright and I promise I'll be strong. I'll do it for Michael as he would have done the same for me if it was someone else's funeral we were arranging.'

Ted was also at the table, although not actively taking part in the conversation, he was there to support them.

He said, 'I'll look after you Muriel. You know you can come to me any time you need a shoulder to cry on.'

'And I will Ted. We all know we can rely on you.' In a kind gesture she put her warm hand on his arm, and squeezed it firmly. His passion was aroused instantly. She had never touched him so tenderly before and he found it hard not to respond affectionately.

The arrangements were discussed, leaving Jack and Margaret to arrange with the funeral directors their wishes for Michael's final journey. They agreed that a private family funeral and burial were to be held in St Peter's Church, Martindale. A memorial service would be arranged at a later date, to be held by the lake, close to where Michael spent so many happy hours. It was planned to be a celebration of his life.

❧ ❧ ❧

Muriel never went back to school. She felt her priority was at home caring for her increasingly frail mother while Jack and Ted continued working the farm. It was one of the busiest times on the farm. Shearing was due to start, and the fields were to be cut gathered and stored for winter feed. It was a tiring time but they pulled together and coped.

Several weeks later Muriel and Ted felt strong enough to begin to plan the memorial service. Jack and Margaret agreed it was time for the service to go ahead but left the planning to the younger ones. Ted and Muriel sat comfortably together on the sofa. The day's last sunshine was shining through the lounge window. Ted sipped a cold beer and Muriel took the lead with pen and paper in hand.

'Right, first we need to choose the date and time, then the venue. I'd like to hold the service on the campsite near the sailing club if they are willing to let us use an area of it for a few hours. We would need to arrange a small seating area for my parents and we need to ask Reverend Jones if he'll conduct the service.'

'Do you think we might need a loudspeaker system?'

'That would be a good idea. We want everyone to hear so they can join in but I have no idea where we could borrow one from.'

Ted recalled that the head teacher had offered help, if the family needed it, and asked Muriel if the school had a loudspeaker system.

'Yes we used one for sports days and anything held in the open air. I wonder if we went to the school they would lend it to us?'

'We'll check it out. Now what else do we need?' asked Ted.

'Obviously a service sheet which we said we'd prepare together. I'm wondering about how many we will need, and the printing cost.'

'I think the school might also be willing to help us with that.'

'You could be right. I think those are the things we need to make personal visits to ask about. I'd like the service sheet to be headed, 'A celebration in memory of the life of Michael Longstaffe' with a photograph of him on the front. The rest we can agree on together.'

Ted was pleased that they were happy for him to help plan such an important service. He and Muriel spent several nights making sure the ceremony would be to everyone's satisfaction. At times emotions ran high, too high for them to continue, and they had to leave off until another time. Eventually they were happy it was coming together as planned.

The campsite owners were willing to section off a large part of their field for the service, even though it meant they would lose business as it was the height of the season. The family knew how popular Michael had been and that many people would want to attend. The date was arranged for Saturday afternoon, 23rd August. Reverend Jones was happy to conduct the service, opening with a prayer to be followed by Michael's favourite childhood hymn, *All things Bright and Beautiful.* The grammar school arranged the printing of the service sheets and the loan of the loudspeaker system which they also helped to install. Mr Fletcher, knowing that with school staff and students alone this would be a large gathering, was happy to oblige.

Tension grew as the day drew closer, and Muriel worried that her mother might not be able to make it, as she had been so ill. Michael's untimely death had rapidly worsened her condition, with the result she had to spend even more of her time in bed. She was well looked after, and was given lots of help and encouragement from family and friends to attend the service.

Muriel said, 'There will be lots of people who would like to see you again Mam and be able to offer their condolences to you personally, people who have known you and Dad for years.' She knew Muriel was right and promised she would make it.

'I must do this for Michael even if it kills me,' she told herself. They understood how difficult it would be, but knew she would regret it until her dying day if she couldn't attend.

Finally the day arrived. The sun shone brightly that morning in a cloudless sky, a reminder of how beautiful the weather had been on the day Michael died. They agreed not to wear black and instead wore subtle colours as Michael would have wanted. He had never been a dull person, always looking on the bright side of life, and if he had been consulted, he would want the ceremony to be a day to remember him as he was.

When they arrived the family were overwhelmed to see how many people had turned up, and were welcomed by Reverend Jones who took them to the seating area. The service began with a prayer followed by Michael's favourite hymn. They later heard that the singing resounded round the lake and fells, it was sung so enthusiastically by the huge crowd who had spilled out across the field. They were joined by campers and passers by who hadn't known Michael. Unbeknown to Jack, Margaret or Muriel, Ted had arranged with Revd. Jones to read a short tribute to Michael's life.

Ted began, 'Michael was to his family a wonderful son, grandson and brother. He became to me like the brother I never had. Along with Philip Brown he had become a possible future Olympic champion and hoped one day that they would both make their families and Cumbria proud. He tragically lost his young life to the same disease his mother is suffering but that no-one had ever suspected. He was so fit and healthy or so everyone thought, even he himself could not have been aware of it. He was taken so cruelly by a heart attack that was so severe we are told even if he had been on land when it happened nothing could have prevented this tragedy.'

He continued to speak of Michael's academic achievements, how all he ever wanted was to be an Olympic competitor alongside Philip. He mentioned how grateful he had been to his family for allowing him the opportunity, always promising that one day he would follow in his father's footsteps and run the farm full time. Then, on behalf of the family, he thanked everyone for coming along and making their day so special, finally saying, 'Michael will be looking down on us now and he will be overwhelmed by the love you have all shown for him today.'

Acknowledging Revd. Jones, Ted stepped down from the makeshift podium in order for the vicar to conclude the service. There was hardly a dry eye to be seen, and when he had finished Muriel dashed over to him and flung her arms around his neck. She was lost for words, tears streamed down her face. For Ted this gesture meant so much – her warm tears against his cheeks gave him great comfort. This had not been easy for him but he felt he owed so much to Muriel's family it was the least he could do in return. Taking her by the hand he led her back to her parents who quietly thanked him. When the service was over, many people came to offer their condolences. It had been a long and tiring day, but one that would live on in their memories forever.

Back at the farm Jack opened a bottle of whisky and poured them all a small tot, insisting that Margaret and Muriel had at least a tiny sip. He held his glass to Ted's and with moist eyes and a lump which felt the size of an egg in his throat, he managed to say a few words.

'Ted, we cannot thank you enough for everything you have done during what has been the most difficult time of our lives. We would have struggled to have coped without you. You will always be very special to us and you are a real part of our family. We hope that you'll continue living and working with us for years to come.'

If only Jack knew how much this was Ted's wish too.

'I hope that will be the case Jack. The years here have been the happiest of my life despite all the pain we have suffered losing Michael.'

※ ※ ※

The day finally ended. Jack made his way wearily up the stairs to join his wife who had already been in bed for a couple of hours, leaving Muriel and Ted together downstairs.

He thought to himself, 'I know she is still very young, and perhaps I shouldn't encourage it, but I can see a bond forming between those two. Everything Ted has done to support her during these past weeks has brought them very close together. Perhaps I am wrong, but I know one thing I would not put a stop to it, and time will tell in the months to come if there is to be something other than a friendly sort of love. She will struggle to find a kinder more caring man who I know would do anything to make her happy.' Then switching off the light he nestled into bed and at last found peace through sleep.

Chapter Thirteen

Time is said to be a healer, but Margaret never got over the death of her only son and within months of Michael's death Margaret's health took a further turn for the worse and she needed to have someone with her most of the time. Jack struggled to believe Michael was dead, but with the farm to run and Margaret to worry over he managed to keep his personal pain hidden from everyone. Muriel gave up her dream to become a veterinary nurse, as she planned to look after her mother and the running of the home. As Scott found it difficult knowing how to handle such a sad situation at the same time as sitting his exams, he and Muriel drifted apart, both thinking that they might meet up again in the future.

Muriel's dreams seemed over for the foreseeable future, but Jack's dream for his daughter's future happiness continued. He felt guilty that Muriel had to put her career on hold but she told him, 'Dad I'm the only Longstaffe left now to keep the farm in the family, so whatever it takes I'll make sure that it never has to be sold to someone else who may change it. I'll make sure that it remains as it has always been a Herdwick sheep farm.'

'It's too tough a job for a woman to run on her own. I know we have Ted but if he ever decides to move on what will you do?' her father asked. Talking to his daughter, Jack was amazed at how mature she was for her age, and how well she had coped with the loss of Michael and her mother's health. He worried that she was burying her head in the sand and one day she would break down completely and find she could no longer carry such a heavy weight on her young shoulders.

'I know that Ted will never leave the farm, certainly not as long as it is owned by a Longstaffe.'

He wondered how she could be so sure of this as, although he knew they were close, he had not noticed any intimate conversations between them. 'What if she were to meet someone else and want to marry and bring her husband to live here and run the farm with her?' he would ask himself. 'Ted seems to belong here with all the time he has lived and worked for us, and if she met someone else she might ask Ted to leave.'

These thoughts unsettled him and he gradually became weary from the worry of everything. He and Margaret were not getting any younger and he knew his wife's days were numbered. He carried a lot of guilt on his shoulders over his daughter having to care for the home, two men and her mother. Muriel loved her life on the farm, and was prepared to sacrifice her dream for her family. She had lost her beloved brother who was unable to fulfil his dream, so she had decided she was prepared to forgo her own in order to see her parents have as comfortable a life as possible.

⚜ ⚜ ⚜

Time moved on and Jack knew that he and Margaret needed to see their solicitor to revise the will. He made the necessary arrangements for it to be done in their own home, as it was difficult for Margaret to travel. They arranged a suitable date, and planned that Muriel and Ted would be out on the fell when the solicitor was due to arrive. Charles & Charles Westbridge had been the family solicitors for Jack's parents before him. Charles senior was now retired and Charles junior was dealing with all their legal business. Arriving promptly, Jack met him at the door.

'Morning Jack nice to see you again. It's a lovely day again a bit chilly but it can be expected at this time of year, and of course, makes for a pleasant drive over from Penrith on a morning like this.'

'It certainly is. Come in Charles it's nice and warm in here and Margaret is up and dressed and ready to do business. She's tired as is to be expected, but this needs to be done and the sooner the better as it won't be easy for us.' Sitting at the table Jack began explaining the changes he and Margaret wanted to make to their will.

'It will remain the same for the most part. The farm going to either Margaret or myself as before.' Jack tactfully omitted the words 'whoever is the surviving partner' and did not even glance across at his wife.

'Of course, Michael's share of the farm will now go to Muriel who, when we have both passed on, will become the sole inheritor. Any outstanding debts are to be settled immediately. The accountant will no doubt work alongside you for that. There are a few extras we wish to be included. Firstly we would like £1,000 to go to our employee Edward Thornton whether he has remained in our employ or not, then £200 each to Philip Brown at the Glenridding Canoe Club, Outward Bound Lake Rescue, the Howtown Outdoor Centre, and Penrith Grammar School. Also, we would like a clause saying that should Muriel choose to marry and her husband comes to live here on the farm, then Edward Thornton, if he is still working for us, must be allowed to remain here in full time employment, living on the farm unless he himself chooses do otherwise.'

'That's a bold statement Jack. Muriel might resent that sort of tie. Have you both thought that out?' He looked across to Margaret who confirmed what Jack had just said.

'That's our wish Charles. Ted has been like a second son to us and the last thing we would want is to see him turned off the farm. We know Muriel would never turn him away, but who knows what could happen. Her husband might think it's his right to override his wife's decision even though the farm belongs to her.'

'Then I shall make sure that clause is included. Now are there any other changes you wish to make before I head off?'

Margaret opened a small notepad and read through the list of changes which they knew almost off by heart, making sure that everything they had written down had been discussed.

'Yes, all done Charles, are you happy with everything Jack?'

Jack agreed with his wife while Charles picked up his briefcase and put his notes inside. On his way to the door he told them that he would return with a copy of the new will within the next week or two for their signatures.

'I will give you a ring and arrange a date and time that's convenient for you both.'

Margaret thanked him as he shook her hand, and watched as Jack saw him out. When he returned to the kitchen he sat down next to his wife and clasping his large rough hands over hers, he saw she was relieved that the task was over.

'Well that's it over, Margaret and not before time. We both know we should have done this sooner but knew how difficult it was going to be.

Now it's sorted we don't have to worry about it any more.'

'Yes, thank goodness one worry less. It gives me peace of mind knowing everything will be properly signed and sealed. If only Michael had shown some signs of having a bad heart he would probably still be with us today. The doctors could have treated him in the same way they have looked after me.' Finding it painful to talk about, her voice softened and her breathing became shallow as she asked Jack to make her a cup of tea before she went to bed for an earlier than usual rest.

Not long after Charles Westbridge had left, Muriel and Ted returned from the fell where they had checked for stray or trapped sheep completely oblivious that anyone had visited the farm that day or that anything official had taken place. When they asked about Margaret, Jack simply said she was fine but felt she needed to take an earlier rest.

It was only eight weeks after the will had been changed that Margaret died. Her death was hastened, the doctor said, from the shock and loss of Michael. She died at home with the family around her and, as with Michael a service and burial was held at St Peter's Church attended by family and friends. She was laid to rest privately in the family grave where she was beside her beloved son. As the family left the churchyard they were overcome with mixed emotions of both sadness and peace. The sadness of losing a wife and mother, but of peace that she was free from her suffering, and that Michael was no longer alone and had his precious mother alongside him.

Back at the farmhouse, Jack wondered what would become of them now. Would Muriel wish to take up her studies again or would she, as she had said, continue to help run the home and farm? She would have so much more time on her hands now that she no longer had to nurse her mother. 'Time will tell Jack, time will tell,' he sighed wearily to himself. His bones seemed to be aching and stiff now, and he was tired after years of hard work and the grief of losing his loved ones. But, he would not give up, and was happy to work alongside Ted when he was needed. That evening Jack left a little earlier than usual in order to get a good night's rest.

'I'll say goodnight and head for my bed. It has been another difficult day for us all, and thanks again for everything you've done. I will leave you to it. Help yourselves to a drink if you'd like one.' He kissed

Muriel, ruffled Ted's hair, and closed the door quietly behind him.

✢ ✢ ✢

Ted had fallen in love with Muriel long before Michael died, and he longed to tell her, but tonight he felt was probably not the right time. He poured another drink and looked across at her, eyes swollen from all the crying. He suddenly knew he could not hide his secret any longer. He yearned to comfort her and held his arms out towards her, 'If you feel it's not right and you'd prefer to be alone with your thoughts I understand.' He was beginning to believe there would come a time when he would take her firmly in his arms and hold her lovingly so, he felt there was no need to rush things. Having waited all this time he could wait a while longer. 'Neither of us are going anywhere,' he told himself, 'and I am sure it will happen one day.'

Muriel did not reject him, but moved slowly towards him and, as he put his arms firmly around her, she knew she loved him too. It was so long since she had seen Scott, and she had almost forgotten the wonderful feeling of being held so closely. She feared at first that her love for Ted was the kind of brotherly love she had felt for Michael, but as they held each other, she knew there was something different, more passionate, about the way she felt about Ted.

'Don't feel you have to do this Muriel, if you're unsure,' Ted said.

'Just hold me tight Ted, please. I need this as much as you do.' She rested her tired body heavily into his, and realised she had wanted him to hold her more than she could have imagined.

Ted gently put his finger under her chin and, lifting her face towards his, he looked into her eyes. He knew she wouldn't push him away and he kissed her, 'I've loved you for so long Muriel. I thought this day would never come. My secret has been so hard to hide but at last I have you in my arms.'

He led her to the sitting room and closed the door behind them. They sat on the sofa and talked quietly so they would not wake Jack. They had seen Muriel's mother buried earlier in the day, and her father needed to rest. As they embraced they talked over the tragic loss of Michael and Muriel's mother and what the future might hold. Ted assured her that he would be there for her whenever she needed him. They talked and cuddled for a couple of hours and were aware that this was the beginning of a different relationship between them. The clock chimed 1.15am and they knew it was time to part company. Kissing her goodnight, Ted said, 'I'll look after you for the rest of your life Muriel, if you will let me.'

She remained silent, stunned by the unexpected events of the evening. She finally answered by returning his kiss. As he crept to his bedroom he wished she was going with him.

CHAPTER FOURTEEN

Ted and Muriel's love for each other grew stronger over time. By then Ted was thirty years old while Muriel was just nineteen and, with the age gap, they felt Jack would never approve, and continued to keep their feelings for each other hidden. Muriel would sometimes wait until her father had gone to bed, soak herself in a perfumed bath, put on clean nightclothes and return downstairs. Ted waited for her, and they spent a relaxing hour or two together, trusting Jack would not reappear.

'We have to make the most of what little time we can, as we have nothing if he tries to keep us apart,' said Ted stroking Muriel's hair, and becoming aroused by the fragrance of her perfume. She looked enticing in her bath robe, silk nightdress and her pink slippers which she kicked off as she sat next to Ted on the sofa. Ted knew he must control his feelings at all costs. They never guessed that Muriel's father wanted them to be together.

Life on the farm slowly returned to normal. He noticed few changes between Ted and his daughter, though sometimes he had his hopes raised. Muriel continued to be housekeeper for the two men in her life whom she loved dearly. She worked hard, cleaning and cooking hearty meals, baking bread and cakes to keep them well fed. Her cooking skills progressed and she spent many happy hours working in the kitchen. Besides running the house she helped around the farm, and did extra work with Ted when her father needed to take things easy. She loved being with Ted, working as a team gave them the opportunity to talk and dream about the day when they hoped to be running the farm together as man and wife.

Muriel had never had time to learn to drive, but her father decided it would be an advantage if she had a driving licence. Rather than her going to a driving school, Ted jumped at the chance to give her lessons saying it would save money. He also knew it would give him an opportunity to spend more time with Muriel. Jack was happy for him to teach her, thinking that the time they were together might bring them closer. 'If it is ever to be, this will be the most likely opportunity for it to happen,' he thought to himself. He felt there had been signs of closeness recently but, fearing disappointment, he continued to disregard the idea. However he tried to arrange opportunities when he could find an excuse to leave them together. Little did he know that Muriel and Ted did not want to tell him for fear of his disapproval.

Driving lessons began after Muriel received her provisional licence, and they spent about and an hour on driving tuition before they found a secluded spot where they could stop to enjoy being alone together. Ted knew plenty of quiet places away from passers-by as he had spent so many years travelling the area while camping. They often discussed how they could tell Jack about their feelings for each another.

'We can't keep it from him forever,' said Ted before kissing her tenderly. She drew closer to him but they had agreed they would go no further until the time and place was right. They wanted the experience to be special and romantic, and this helped them control their feelings.

'I love you so much Muriel. Tell me you will never love anyone else and that you will marry me.'

'You know I will Ted but we'll have to wait until the time is right to tell Dad. He has gone through enough in recent years without us dropping another bombshell on him. I really worry about what he will think.'

'Do you really believe he has no idea at all?'

'I don't think he has. Besides I think he probably has you down as a confirmed bachelor as you've never mentioned girls to any of us, as far as I know, at least not to me anyway.'

'You're right I haven't, but I've had my eye on a beautiful young woman for a long time now.'

'That had better be me you're talking about Ted Thornton!' she joked.

'Of course it is who else would it be! I've watched you mature into the beautiful woman I am holding in my arms right now, yet I thought this day would never come.'

'Muriel Thornton,' then repeating it, 'Mrs Muriel Thornton, yes sounds good to me.'

'Then let's not put off telling your father for much longer. We will wait till he seems to be in good fettle and then we'll sit him down and break the news to him.'

'You're right. We can't keep it from him for much longer, now I think it's time to be getting back before he starts to worry where we are.'

She took the wheel, composed herself and concentrated on her driving as they headed for home.

'I reckon you are ready now to take your driving test Muriel, so if you complete your test application form tonight we can get it sent off as soon as possible. The day you pass your father will be so pleased I think that would be a good time to tell him. What do you think?'

'I think that's a brilliant idea, and it could turn into a double celebration if he is happy to hear our news.'

Jack watched as his daughter drove the car towards him when they arrived back at the farm. Showing off a little she sped along the farm track and brought the car to a halt in its usual place. She jumped out and was beaming. 'That was a good lesson Dad, and Ted says I should put in for my test so I am going to complete the form tonight and get it in the post hopefully tomorrow.'

'The sooner the better I say, no good putting it off if you think you're ready.'

She couldn't wait to get the form in the post. She asked her father to take it along to the main Post Office thinking it would arrive the next day. Jack was oblivious to the real motive behind the urgency, but now it was decided when he was to discover their secret they couldn't wait to tell him and this made her more determined than ever that she must pass her test at the first attempt.

A couple of anxious weeks went past before the brown envelope with the date for her driving test finally arrived.

'It's my driving test date she shouted,' as she tore open the envelope with such enthusiasm she almost tore the document inside. She read the date and time, Tuesday 2nd May at 12 noon. Grabbing the calendar she wrote, 'Driving Test at 12' against the date with two question marks alongside. One referring to passing her test, and the other to breaking the news to her father of their love. Would they be able to break two lots of good news in one day? She hoped so, then counting from that day, it meant waiting two weeks and four days.

'I'll need extra lessons before then to make sure I pass first time,' she said her eyes scanning the expressions on the two men's faces.

'Do you think we'll manage that Jack? We are struggling a bit to fit in one lesson a week at the minute.' Ted was trying to wind her up, as she knew there were only a few ewes still to lamb, and that they were working exceptionally long hours. Jack knew he could free Ted up to give her extra lessons, as he was determined to see her succeed.

'Of course we'll manage somehow Muriel. You may have to cut the time down a bit but even just an hour should help.'

Hardly daring to look Ted in the eye for fear she gave something away she laughed to herself thinking, 'If only he knew we only ever do about an hour driving.'

'Thanks Dad, now you two had best be out from under my feet as I need to get this kitchen sorted out and there are other jobs to be done before lunch.'

At eleven o'clock on the morning of her test Ted set off with his nervous passenger. 'I'll drive to Pooley, and then you take over the wheel for some last minute practice.' He took her hand and said, 'Now calm yourself down because I know that you are well prepared for this and you will not fail.'

'I do hope you're right Ted as it would be such an advantage.'

The remainder of the journey was somewhat subdued as they were both considered what might be the outcome of the day. They had their fingers crossed that they would have lots to celebrate that night. Ted, was organised and had already arranged cover with Dennis and Tom for a couple of hours, and they arrived at the farm before they left. The two lads had agreed to work that night if needed. Jack was rather puzzled by so many changes, but took it in his stride, not questioning but leaving things to Ted.

Ted gave her a peck on the cheek as he left her at the test centre in Carlisle, 'Good luck sweetheart you can do it.' She felt slightly more confident at last.

'I'll do it Ted for us not just for me,' and she headed off in search of the examiner.

During the test Ted planned a trip to the jewellers. Taking one of

Muriel's rings with him for size, he bought her an engagement ring. He thought, 'I know she'll pass today, so when we tell Jack tonight I'll surprise them both.'

With the boxed diamond ring safely zipped inside one of his pockets he returned to the test centre, confident Muriel would have passed. He hoped, with Jack's blessing, he could propose to her later that evening.

He waited ten minutes until he spotted the car pulling over. When she had parked, he watched as the examiner spoke to her, handed her a piece of paper and they shook hands. The door opened, Muriel spotted Ted and ran towards him shouting, 'I did it, I've passed, I've passed!'

'I knew you would,' he said, hugging and congratulating her, his heart pounding he was so pleased. His thoughts raced ahead to Jack, and his planned speech, 'Please tell us it would make you a very happy man to see us together, then I will ask if I can have your daughter's hand in marriage, and slip this engagement ring onto her finger.'

Ted insisted he drove the car back, as she was too excited to pay full attention to driving. Jack was waiting for them at the door when they returned and, although she got out of the passenger seat, he knew that she had passed by the happy smiles. Muriel threw her 'L' plates into the air shouting, 'I did it Dad! I did it! Are you proud of me?'

'Of course I am, and we never ever doubted you would pass did we Ted?' He gave her a big hug, 'We'll leave the celebrations until tonight when we can all enjoy a drink, if we get the lads to look after the lambing for us. We've had a set of twin lambs born while you were out so we can look forward to a double celebration tonight.'

'Even a triple hopefully,' Muriel whispered to Ted.

Ted winked at her, and without bothering to change back into his farm clothes, he went straight over to see the new born twins.

'I'll be over to see them as soon as I've prepared dinner. Let's hope the ewe doesn't reject them - make sure you let me know Ted.' He was gone without an answer, the job must come first. He wanted to check that all three were okay.

Overwhelmed by the events of the day, Muriel raced upstairs and changed her clothes. She thought, 'I'll have to cook something special tonight, something I know Dad really enjoys as I have a feeling everything is going to turn out just right. I can see Dad is very happy for me

108

just as Ted said he would be, and with the arrival of more twin lambs surely he will be pleased with our news.'

She took her mother's tattered and slightly faded handwritten book of recipes from the shelf and looked for her father's favourite. She decided for Ted it would be his favourite starter, 'I need to please them both' she reminded herself and for the main course her father's favourite, which her mother had named Jack's shepherd's pie. The gravy had to be made in a certain way with a generous dash of Worcestershire sauce. She remembered her mother had always served the pie with herby dumplings, carrots and swede. Finally for pudding she chose one of her mother's favourites, an orange and lemon cheesecake. Preparations for the meal were nicely started when Ted appeared in the kitchen.

'Everything's fine across there and there is another ewe lambing as I left, so do make time to pop down to see them.'

'I'm too busy at the moment. I'm planning a special meal for tonight.'

'Sounds good to me, but be careful we don't want to be giving your father too many surprises in one day.'

'Oh and by the way, I have made a few sandwiches for you to take back with you. I'm not planning dinner until after seven so you will need something to eat before then.'

She turned to carry on with her preparations and Ted planted a kiss on the back of her neck before he headed upstairs. Five minutes later he was back, picked up the food, took a bottle of lemonade from the cupboard and seconds later he was off whistling a happy tune to see if the lambs had arrived.

Listening to him through the open kitchen window she smiled and thought, 'I do love you Ted Thornton, and I hope our dreams are not dashed tonight because I can't begin to imagine how we will take it if it turns out that Dad is totally against the idea.'

Several hours later she dressed in her favourite blue jeans and a new pale blue sleeveless top, her long hair loose over her slender tanned shoulders. She entered the kitchen slightly nervous, wondering what the two men in her life would have to say. Ted admired her in silence while Jack looked with pride at his daughter who, he thought, had matured so beautifully.

'My you do look lovely tonight Muriel, as does the table. It's a long time since it was set so beautifully with flowers and candles, wine glasses and the best place mats.' He thought, 'She seems to have gone to extremes tonight to celebrate passing her driving test.'

She replied blushing slightly, 'It's a special occasion. I passed my driving test and we have our third set of twin lambs today.'

'I guess you're right lass, perhaps we should do something like this more often. It's so easy to get stuck in a rut doing things the same way day in and day out. We shouldn't have to wait until there is something to celebrate to have a special meal together.'

First course was on the table and Ted filled the wine glasses. Muriel and Ted glanced at one another waiting to speak to Jack. They had planned that Ted would give a sign when he was about to break the news and he waited until Muriel put the pudding plates on the table. He refilled their glasses then giving her a small nod, she knew the time had come. Bracing herself she took a deep breath. Her heart was racing as she sat down and waited for her father's reaction.

'Muriel and I have something special we would like to ask you tonight.'

'Go ahead lad you know me, I'm always ready to listen,' said Jack.

Rather than telling him outright he decided it would be best to put it as a question thinking this way he would have to ponder his thoughts rather than give an immediate response. 'How would you feel if we were to say that, since Margaret passed away, we had become romantically involved?'

Jack sat bolt upright on his chair clasping both hands behind his head. With a broad grin and wide eyed he said, 'Well, well, well you two that's wonderful news. Although I have had my suspicions at times, I can tell you now, you are making me a happier man tonight than I have been for a long, long time. I could not have wished more for my daughter than this and a more reliable couple could not take over the running of the farm.' He paused briefly in order to take in the news, 'If your mother and Michael were alive today, God rest their souls, they would be delighted with your news, and now I think I understand the reason behind this special meal tonight.'

Muriel's eyes filled with tears of happiness. She pushed her chair back, and went over to her father and gave him a long hug.

'You don't know what that means to us. We were worried that you would not approve, with Ted being quite a lot older than me.'

'I'm thrilled for you both, more than you will ever realise,' he said planting a kiss on her cheek.

Muriel returned to her seat and Ted took her hand in his, and turning to Jack asked for his daughter's hand in marriage.

'If that's what you both want then I'll not stand in your way so I guess the answer is a resounding yes.'

Thanking Jack with a handshake, Ted put his hand in his pocket and pulled out the small blue velvet box. He opened it and lifted the ring from the satin lining. His eyes met Muriel's - her face was a picture - she was so surprised. Taking her hand in his he asked, 'Muriel Longstaffe will you marry me?'

Completely overwhelmed at how well everything had turned out, she glanced at her father who was smiling generously, and turning to Ted she leaned over to kiss him. 'Of course I will Ted Thornton. You know how much I love you.' Ted put the ring on her finger.

This was the first time Jack had seen any romantic contact between them and he was moved. Taken aback by the events of the evening, he realised he ought to propose a toast and picking up his glass, gestured to the newly engaged couple that they do the same.

'I wish you both all the happiness you deserve, and hope that you will be content with your life together as much as your mother and I were.'

'We hope we will be Dad, and thanks for being so happy for us and being here to share this with us. I just wish Mam and Michael were here too.' Then raising her glass, 'We all miss you both so much. I hope you are looking down on us and sharing in our happiness tonight.'

'I'm sure they are my love, I'm sure they are.' These were Jack's only sorrowful words, as he enjoyed the celebrations with the two people left in his world who meant so much to him.

CHAPTER FIFTEEN

The wedding took place on the 10 November. Jack would have liked his daughter to have married at St. Peter's Church but Muriel could not face the thought of her beloved mother and brother lying only a few feet away on her wedding day. After several discussions they decided on a quiet wedding at Gretna Green. It was not their preferred venue, nor was it their wish to be married without family and friends present, but unable to face the day without her mother and Michael, Muriel decided this was best. Jack was sad but understood the decision, and Ted's parents, delighted with the news their son was to be married, respected the couple's wishes. Jack said he would manage without them for a few days so they planned a brief honeymoon in Scotland. They refused to leave him for more than one night but, at his insistence, they finally agreed to stay for three.

The day arrived and they dressed in their wedding outfits before leaving as the venue was less than two hours away, and they wanted Jack to see them in their outfits before they left. Muriel chose the same colours her mother had worn when she was married - a pale blue dress with matching jacket, and navy blue accessories. She wore around her neck on a gold chain her mother's treasured wedding ring which she had given to her just days before she died. She also carried a small bouquet of silk flowers in blues, white and yellows. Ted wore a navy pinstripe suit, white shirt and pale blue tie with a yellow carnation pinned to his lapel. Jack gave them his blessing and thought what a wonderful couple they made. They said goodbye and they could see he was truly happy.

'Well Dad we will be Mr and Mrs Thornton in a few hours from now,' Muriel announced as though he needed to be reminded. Kissing him goodbye, she saw he was quite emotional and crossed quickly to the car where Ted was ready to go, having half suspected the happy occasion could turn into a tearful departure.

They married in a brief ceremony in the Old Blacksmith's Shop beside the famous Old Smithy Marriage Anvil. Jack had given them an envelope which they were told was not to be opened until after the ceremony. They knew it would tell them about the honeymoon but had no idea where it would be. When they opened the envelope, they found the front cover torn from a Gardens Hotel brochure where they were to spend their honeymoon. This was Jack's gift to them and they were speechless for a few moments as they admired the building with its beautiful surroundings. Neither of them had ever stayed in such an exquisite place and they were grateful at the expense Jack had gone to, to make sure their honeymoon was special. Ted drove to the hotel and parked the car. They went in through the revolving glass doors to the reception area where they had a warm welcome from an immaculately dressed receptionist.

'Good afternoon, Mr and Mrs Thornton I presume?'

'It is,' Ted replied and turning to Muriel he could see the words had brought a slight colour to her cheeks. Although not normally a shy person, Muriel felt slightly embarrassed. Ted drew her towards him in a gesture that seemed to say, 'Don't be embarrassed hundreds of newly weds have spent their honeymoon in this hotel and the staff are used to this.'

'We hope you will enjoy your stay with us. I see that you are booked in for three nights, bed, breakfast and evening meal. A table has been reserved for you in the Terrace Restaurant at 8 o'clock this evening and breakfast is served between 7.30 and 9.30. The porter will take your bags to your room for you.

Muriel still slightly embarrassed, felt she wanted to be included in the conversation and replied, 'That will be lovely thank you very much.'

'We look forward to seeing you this evening and should you require anything further there's a telephone in your room direct to reception.' Having completed the formalities and, with the arrivals book signed by Mr and Mrs Thornton, the receptionist handed them their room keys with a tag reading 'the bridal suite' and gave them directions.

Overwhelmed by the extravagance of it all, Ted thanked the receptionist again before they went to the lift. Although they had shared the same house for several years, and knew each other well, they had never shared the same bedroom and Ted was aware Muriel was feeling a little nervous. He held her hand tightly as he unlocked the door and, without any warning, swept her off her feet and carried her over the threshold.

They were delighted by the room, its size, and its beautiful furnishings. There was a wonderful fragrance from a bouquet of flowers arranged perfectly on the polished table. Next to this was a bottle of champagne with two glistening champagne flutes on a silver tray. Several envelopes addressed to them at the hotel were laid alongside and they began excitedly to open them. They wondered who they could be from as they thought only Muriel's father and Ted's parents knew about the wedding. There were several cards from people who had known Muriel all her life who Jack had proudly informed of his daughter's forthcoming marriage.

'It's clear that Dad has told someone about our wedding and word has got around and here's us thinking no-one knew! Never mind, it is a lovely surprise to receive all these cards and as Dad was so pleased for us it's little wonder he could not keep it to himself.'

The cards included one from the hotel congratulating them on their marriage and wishing them a pleasant stay. Another came from Ted's parents with a cheque for £200 as a wedding gift. Finally only one card remained which Muriel had purposely put to the bottom of the pile, when she recognised the handwriting. The card was from her father wishing them a happy, healthy and successful marriage. He signed it, 'With love to my beautiful daughter Muriel and Ted my wonderful son-in-law, Dad, x x x.'

They both felt sad about Muriel's mother and Michael's missing names, but realised that her father had sent three kisses, one from each of them. Tears welled up in their eyes as they spoke of how they wished all the family could have been with them. Ted held her in his arms and diverted her attention when he opened the champagne. Muriel tried her best to hide her pain and suggested they look around the rest of the bridal suite which was the size of two or three rooms. They looked at the bathroom, where they found a shining white bath with shower and gold coloured taps. There were soft peach coloured towels, with white bathrobes embroidered in peach with 'his' and 'hers' across the pockets. Bottles of expensive toiletries and bowls of pot pourri were neatly placed near the bath. The curtains and carpet were in the same shade of peach and gave the bathroom a warm, relaxing, feel.

Muriel and Ted were delighted by the bedroom where there was a king-size four poster bed - the sort of bed they had never seen before except in magazines. The bedspread, carpet and curtains were of shades of a creamy colour with dark wood furniture. There were pretty floral pictures on the walls, matching bedside lamps and a small box of chocolates. Muriel thought the room was delightful and appreciated why her father had taken so much trouble to make their stay a dream come true.

'I can't believe how kind Dad has been, going to this expense for us,' Muriel's voice trembled with excitement as she took Ted's hand and pulled him onto the bed. Ted turned towards his beautiful wife and kissed her more passionately than he had ever done before knowing he no longer had to control his desire.

'At last you're all mine,' he whispered.

✄ ✄ ✄

They fell asleep and two hours later woke surprised by the darkness of the room. The autumn sun had set, and the darkening evening sky showed through the window. Street lamps and car headlights shone in the distance.

They unpacked, bathed and dressed for the evening meal. Everything finally unpacked and ready, Ted opened the champagne and filled their glasses.

'I love you so much Ted I don't know what I would have done without you during the past few years.'

He put his finger on her lips to silence her as he did not want her to dwell on her losses. He put his hand beneath her chin, raised her face towards his and kissed her once more.

A few hours later after their meal, they left the hotel to take a short walk for some fresh air. They intended to take a romantic stroll around the floodlit gardens but it turned into a brisk walk. The evening was damp and autumnal so they returned to the warmth of the hotel, where they enjoyed a few glasses of wine followed by a night cap of coffee and brandy, before heading back to their rooms. It had been a perfect day from beginning to end.

The honeymoon was soon over, but they could not have been happier. The November days remained dry and sunny, and they enjoyed visits to some of the local attractions, taking in the glorious sights and colours of autumn before it was time to return home. Jack welcomed them with open arms saying he had missed them and was glad to have them back at the farm. 'It hasn't been the same place without you.'

'It's nice to be back. We'll be with you in just a few minutes after we have taken our cases upstairs.'

'No rush, take your time, I'll see you when you come down,' Jack smiled to himself as he had left a further surprise for them upstairs.

When she went into her bedroom Muriel was taken aback and called to Ted. 'Come here quick and see what Dad's done.' Standing at the door Ted saw that Jack had replaced Muriel's single bed with a new double bed, and a set of bedding in matching colours which had completely transformed the room. It had become a bedroom to share. They dashed back downstairs and Muriel was greeted with a huge smile on her father's face as she gave him a big hug.

'Oh Dad it's lovely, thank you so much,' and, after a brief pause she asked, 'you must have had that all arranged before we left?'

'Let's say I might have done, and it's thanks to the assistant in the bedding department who chose the colours when I had described the room to her, that it looks so nice. I could never have done it on my own.'

Ted said, 'We don't know how to thank you enough for your generous gifts. Our honeymoon hotel was wonderful, and to come home to this, well what can I say?'

'You don't have to say anything. If anyone deserved a treat it's you two after all you've both done. Now let's open the champagne I have ready on ice, and drink to your future. I still have a few jobs that must be done before we all get dressed for dinner at the Water View Hotel where your mother and I celebrated our wedding.'

He watched the disbelief on their faces, but he was the one getting the most pleasure from the day. Seeing Muriel and Ted happy meant more than anything else to him. Since losing his wife and son Muriel's happiness was the most important thing in his life, and at last he could sleep at night knowing that Ted would never let her down.

'The table is booked for 7pm, as I've not had a decent meal inside me since my number one cook left for a wedding causing me to lose a few pounds in weight.' The laughter echoed from the walls and Felix Hill farmhouse was rejuvenated with happiness.

Another treat was almost too much, but they were delighted that they would be sharing a family meal. Ted said there would be no arguments and he would do the driving so Jack could enjoy a few drinks to celebrate. Toasting their marriage that night, Muriel and Ted could not have imagined that yet more good fortune had come their way. Among the unopened mail in the small wicker tray that sat on the corner of the kitchen cupboard was a letter addressed 'Private and Confidential' to Mr Edward Thornton.

The white envelope had a company logo printed in the top left hand corner which read, 'Watson and Hay Solicitors, Grey Street, Newcastle-upon-Tyne. The postmark showed 9 November so the letter had arrived at Felix Hill not long after Ted and Muriel had set off for Gretna Green.

Jack had been curious as to what news the envelope might contain, but did not hurry to point out to Ted that there was a letter for him. Unopened mail could wait until the following morning as they were too excited about the wedding and the homecoming. They spent the rest of the day celebrating and nothing was going to interfere with the occasion.

The following morning while cooking breakfast Muriel took the mail from the tray and flicked through checking for letters that might need to be dealt with urgently. She saw Ted's letter and was as curious as her father had been and laid the envelope next to his place on the table knowing he would want to open it. The remaining letters could wait - her only interest was in Ted's unexpected correspondence.

'Whatever can it be?' she pondered. 'Having a Newcastle post mark I hope it's not bad news of someone in his family.'

The kitchen door opened and Jack came in, and saw the letter on the table. He looked at Muriel, 'I wonder what it can be? I didn't want to tell him about it yesterday fearing it was bad news and that would have completely spoilt the rest of our day.'

'Well one thing's certain Dad we will know very soon.' Ted arrived for breakfast and wished them both a cheerful, 'Good morning.' He noticed the kettle boiling on the Aga and carried it to the table and filled the teapot before spotting the letter. Frowning he leaned over and picked it up. 'Whatever can this be? A letter from a solicitor for me, that's strange.' Muriel passed him the letter opener and watched his expression as he opened the envelope and took the letter from inside. His eyes widened as he began reading.

Dear Mr Thornton,
<u>*Re: Mr Thomas Joseph Thornton deceased.*</u>

I am pleased to advise that we have completed the administration for Mr Thornton's estate and I enclose a cheque for £10,000 representing the amount of inheritance due to you.

I would be grateful if you could sign and return the enclosed form to acknowledge its safe receipt.

Yours sincerely,

James Hay, Watson and Hay Solicitors.

Enclosures: One Cheque and one Receipt of Inheritance Payment.

He was unable to speak as his eyes scanned the words over and over until he finally read the letter aloud to his two anxious onlookers. Shocked, not only by the amount of money, but having never heard of this relative, he wondered who he was and why he would leave him an inheritance.

'I can't believe it,' he said, his face pale, his voice trembled and he shook his head in disbelief. 'I've never even heard mother or father mention Thomas Joseph Thornton or that he had any connection to the family. I wonder if they know anything about this, and if they have also received a letter and a cheque?' Everyone was stuck for words though delighted with Ted's news.

Muriel broke the silence and suggested it would be a good idea to eat breakfast before it was overcooked.

'I'm not sure if I can eat anything,' Ted said, still staring at the letter. He didn't raise his head but slowly pulled his chair out and took his place at the table. Ignoring his remark, Muriel put his breakfast in front of him and he picked up his knife and fork and managed to eat, as she knew he would. Breakfast was not as chatty as usual with little said about the day ahead. The content of the letter was beginning to sink in, and for Ted to inherit this legacy left them puzzled. To receive this amount of money from someone he did not even know seemed uncanny. Ted was just about to talk when the telephone rang.

Muriel went to answer and they heard her say, 'Yes thanks it was a lovely day and thank you for your wonderful wedding present, are you both well?'

Though hearing only one side of the conversation Ted knew that it was his mother on the phone.

'Is she ringing to congratulate us or has she also received a letter?' he wondered.

'Yes, yes he has. I'll put him on and I'll speak to you again later.' Muriel passed the phone to Ted. She assumed that his parents had also received a letter as a call early in the morning was unusual.

'Hi Mum, thanks for your card and present. Yes it was wonderful she looked beautiful, and thanks to Jack as you know, we spent our honeymoon in the Gardens Hotel. We'll be popping you some photographs in the post as soon as we have them developed.'

There was silence for several moments while Ted listened to what his mother had to say, and then answering her he began.

'Yes I have, for £10,000. I can't believe it, who was he?' A longer silence followed this time, until eventually Ted replied.

'Really, but neither you nor Dad have ever mentioned him before, or at least not that I can remember.'

The conversation continued for three to four minutes until Ted concluded, 'I'll have to speak to you again later as I really need to get cracking. Work is calling - it's great news and I am pleased that Dad received some money as well.' He put the phone down and returned to the table.

'You'll have guessed they have also received a cheque, for £2,000. Apparently Thomas Joseph was a distant relative on father's side, an intelligent man who worked his way up on the management side of the shipbuilding industry. He kept himself to himself, never bothered with the family, never married and fortunately for us it seems he dabbled in stocks and shares and owned property.'

Jack said, 'Sounds to me like he was a shrewd man who invested well and, even though he didn't keep in touch with his family, he has made sure they benefited from his savings. Very generous of him you must admit. So you make sure you invest your money wisely Ted. Get sound advice so that it brings you good returns when you need it.'

'I think you're right, but I'm still too stunned to take it all in. I will have to take a leaf out of Thomas Joseph's book and, one thing for certain, I won't be wasting it.'

Jack shook his hand, 'This is good news Ted and what a lovely time in your life for it to happen. I'm really happy for you.' Jack then left the kitchen to allow him to share his thoughts with Muriel.

Ted wrapped his arms around her and said, 'I always knew you would be lucky for me Muriel Longstaffe, whoops, sorry Thornton.'

Muriel laughed, 'It's wonderful news for you Ted though rather sad you never met him or even knew about him. Just promise me this, you will never run off and leave me now you have come into some money?'

'As though I would. You know better than anyone that my life is here in Cumbria with you Jack and the farm. Your family changed my life and made me so happy when I came to work here. I wouldn't change it for anything. If an offer to travel the world free arrived in the post tomorrow I wouldn't accept it. I have everything I want right here.'

'That's what I wanted to hear,' she said kissing him. She came back to reality and reminded him they had work to do.

Ted's money remained untouched until he decided on the best way to invest it. He knew he would use it for things to benefit the farm. The years passed quickly and they accepted that they wouldn't have children as Muriel didn't get pregnant. This did not stop them enjoying life as they worked the farm together. Jack had cut back on the work he did, and they knew that one day an extra pair of hands would be needed as they planned changes for the future.

Ted suggested, 'How about us asking your father if we can convert the old barn into a cottage? We could rent it out as a holiday cottage or if we do need help we can offer living accommodation if they need it. I can use the money I have in the bank for the building work, as property is always a good investment, and I'm sure he would agree to it don't you?'

'What a brilliant idea. I'm sure Dad would be happy to go along with that if we can get plans passed for a conversion, and it would mean that we will no longer have to go on sharing the house with others. We have lived with family for as long as we have known each other, though I can't imagine what it would be like just two of us living in the house. A cottage I'm sure will be a sensible investment for our future so we'll talk it over.'

The council passed the planning application and the barn was converted into a two bedroom cottage, named Felix Cottage. Ted helped with the work to keep the cost down and Muriel helped where she could. Jack did his bit when he felt strong enough, but the greatest help he gave was financial. He offered a substantial amount towards the conversion, by paying money into the joint account and updated his will to include that, following his death the farm and cottage were to be jointly owned by Ted and Muriel. He was certain that Ted would never let his daughter down.

Jack died during the winter and was buried beside his wife and son. Ted and Muriel were sad but their work on the farm kept their thoughts away from the past. In the years that followed they invested in the farm. The priority was to modernise the farmhouse so central heating was installed. A modern kitchen replaced the antiquated pantry, worn out cupboards and worktops. The Aga and original fireplace were kept, but a small area of the kitchen was separated off as a utility room and downstairs cloakroom. Upstairs two bedrooms were knocked into one, to make room for an extra bathroom.

The sheep remained the prime source of income, but Muriel planned how the farm could make extra income to maintain the farm and the houses. She decided to keep a larger number of hens, to sell the eggs locally. Ted and Muriel's love of collies became an investment when they decided to breed them and sell some of the pups. Ted agreed a small stable could be built and rented out with one of the fields for further income. When they could they worked as a team devoted to each other and to the farm, ensuring it would prosper and be a business Muriel's late parents and brother would have been proud of.

'If only Mam, Dad and Michael were here to see the farm now they would never believe it!' These were words often spoken as they happily went about their lives.

CHAPTER SIXTEEN

Muriel sobbed relentlessly for what seemed hours but finally managed to lift herself from the bedroom chair and crossed to the window. The clouds had darkened and she heard the wind whistling around the farmhouse and saw the trees swaying violently from side to side. She checked the time; it was past mid-day and her thoughts went back to the three men knowing how hazardous it would be up on the fell. 'Hopefully they should be on their way down before it gets much worse,' she told herself, as she turned back to the window wishing they had never had to make the journey at all that day.

She was surprised to see Sheila's car coming up the track, having completely forgotten about inviting her for lunch, as she had re-lived in her memory, the terrible day when her beloved brother lost his life. She tried to reduce her swollen eyes by splashing them with cold water before she went downstairs. She heard Bess barking to warn her someone was approaching as she brushed her hair which was damp and untidy, from her tear-drenched fingers running through it so many times. By the time she reached the bottom of the stairs she heard Sheila calling as she opened the door.

'It's just me I'm here at last.' When she saw Muriel she was taken aback and her tone of voice changed, 'Oh Muriel whatever's the matter?'

'It's nothing Sheila I'll be okay in a few minutes.'

'I knew there was something wrong when I spoke to you earlier, even Brenda could tell by my voice that something was wrong and that's why she suggested I finish a little earlier. She knew I needed to check on Tia first and that I wanted to get to you as soon as possible.'

'Oh I'll be alright Sheila but as you can see I haven't made our lunch yet. I happened to pick up Michael's photograph to dust as I do most days, but for some reason today I became really upset remembering that terrible day. Perhaps I shouldn't tell you this...' She hesitated thinking it would be better not to go over her anxieties.

'You shouldn't tell me what?' Sheila was anxious to know exactly what was going on in her best friend's head.

'Oh nothing, it's probably me just being silly and imagining things.'

'Muriel I need to know what's worrying you if I'm to be of any help. You can't expect me to just sit here and not do anything seeing you this distraught. It can't be nothing.'

Muriel pondered before she hesitantly confessed her concerns. 'I have had a horrible feeling all morning that there's going to be another awful accident today, and seeing Michael's photo brought back memories of just what a horrendous experience it was to have to go through. I just seemed to lose control, knowing I couldn't face going through another day like that. Tell me Sheila, I'm just being stupid and that nothing is going to happen?'

Sheila hesitated before replying as the worsening weather was concerning her too. She didn't want to upset Muriel any more than she already was and needed to choose her words carefully. Sheila had become friends when she moved into Felix Cottage. She knew their friendship was invaluable, and nothing they had ever said had offended the other, but 'today may be different' she feared. They were always comfortable in each other's company, and never afraid to tell each other what was on their minds. Sheila knew how sensitive Muriel was when she thought about Michael's death, and she needed comfort and reassurance.

'Everything will be just fine Muriel, you'll see. I realise the weather is getting worse and much earlier in the day than the forecast predicted, but those men of ours are tough and know the fells like the backs of their hands. Even Stephen, though he has never brought the sheep down, has spent his life walking the fells from being a young lad and knows pretty well how to handle himself whilst he's up there.' She went to Muriel, put a comforting arm around her shoulder and gave her a hug. 'Now come on stop all the worrying. How about putting the kettle on for a cup of tea and while it's boiling I'll make us a sandwich.'

'I guess you're right Sheila. There's some ham left over from making Ted's sandwiches this morning. It will be in the fridge. There's enough for us both and you know where the mustard is, but don't put any on mine thanks. Oh and don't salt them as the ham is quite salty.'

'Ok and how many sandwiches would you like, one or two with white or brown bread?'

'Brown bread for me please, and two each if there's enough ham. There are some tomatoes in the fridge if you'd like to add a couple, while I put us some cake out. Gosh that reminds me it's Friday and I need to do the baking this afternoon. I'd almost forgotten with all this silly crying and worrying.'

'Right Muriel let's stop this panicking and, as I said to you on the phone earlier, I'm more than willing to help out this afternoon. While you bake I will do some ironing for you and at the same time we can attempt to put the world to rights.'

Muriel was relieved and happy to accept Sheila's offer. Her routine had been turned upside down, and an extra pair of hands would be appreciated. 'Okay thanks, but just for today if you're sure you can spare the time.'

'For a friend as good as you are to me and my family Muriel, I will always find the time. We owe you and Ted a lot. There are so many things we could never have done but for the help you've given us.'

'Oh don't be silly,' Muriel replied as she put slices of walnut cake from an almost empty tin on a plate. The urgency of this afternoon's baking session suddenly hit her, not only to replenish her empty cake tins, but also for the shops and cafes she supplied ready for their weekend business.

'Good heavens Sheila I'd best get my lunch over quickly and get started on the baking or no-one will be eating or making any money. I think the kettle has boiled so I'll make the tea and then we can sit down but not before I put some coal on the Aga and bring it back to life.'

Thankfully there was enough coal left in the scuttle on the hearth saving her the job of going outside. Bess, laid in her usual position right in front of the fire, despite it not generating much heat was given a stroke. 'Do you think you could possibly move Bess so I can throw some coal on the fire?' After what seemed a struggle she managed to lift herself onto all four legs and edged just far enough away for Muriel to reach the Aga.

'Do you know she would spend the rest of her life on this rug right in front of the Aga.'

'And who can blame her poor lass, when she can't go running around like the others do. It's her bit of luxury.'

'Yes, you're right, we do spoil her and she does get the best of every-thing and, even though she's lost her sight, she still has a good life.'

Muriel brought the kettle back to the boil before she made the tea. 'I'm more than ready for a good cup of tea it seems hours since I had a coffee, shortly after the men left.'

'We had a late ten o'clock break this morning as we were really busy with the bedrooms so I'm not too bad, but you know me Muriel I'm always ready for a nice cup of tea when it's on offer. I did grab a glass of milk and a biscuit at home before I looked in on Tia who was very quiet but didn't look as though she was about to deliver. I suspect that the men will be right and she's nearly sure to have her pups before the day's over.'

'Do you think you'll be keeping any of them?'

'What do you think Muriel? I can't see Stephen parting with them all. He's bound to want to keep one of them, but I tell you this, he can't keep one every time there's a litter. We couldn't possibly afford to keep more than two dogs and besides two is enough to look after even though they have lots of space to run around. I rather think he'll want to train a pup himself to work with the sheep now that he's working on the farm.'

'I think you could be right. Ted will help and he would get lots of sat-isfaction knowing he had trained a dog himself. It takes skill but I know he could do it.'

Chatting away happily throughout their lunch neither of them noticed the time and when Muriel glanced at the clock she leapt from her chair, and suggested that the ironing would have to wait as she could do with some help with the baking.

'I really must get started as I have to have the orders delivered today and I can't let anyone down.'

'Of course I'll help. Let's clear the table and wash the dishes then we will have a clean start. Is everything planned that you are baking today?'

'Yes there's a list next to the letter tray and I have all the ingredients on hand just ready to start.'

Muriel got the ingredients ready while Sheila oiled the baking trays and began weighing flour.

'Let's not forget the oven - will it be hot enough?' Sheila asked.

Muriel's mind still seemed only half on the job at hand.

'Thanks for the reminder - I think the Aga is hot enough though.' Muriel remembered most of the recipes so did not need to check for quantities, temperatures or cooking times. The Friday order was routine so she knew which cakes and pastries had to be baked and delivered to which shop or cafe. The baking session helped keep their minds from worrying about the men out on the fells, but it was not long before they had to put the lights on as the skies were darkening and the wind was whistling down the chimney. Intentional or not neither of them mentioned the weather until a sudden squall lashed rain against the kitchen window.

Muriel commented, 'Well we expected it even though I had wished it would have held off until later. Those poor men of ours out in that while we are warm and cosy in the kitchen.'

'I'm sure they'll be fine and they are nearly certain to be down on the in-bye land by now.'

'I reckon they should be. While you are next to the oven Sheila can you lift that last tray of scones out for me before they start to burn?'

'My pleasure. Cheese scones are my favourite and I'd hate to see trays of them blackened - what a waste that would be.'

When the baking was finished the kitchen table and dresser were covered with pastries, scones and cakes. Muriel asked, 'If you put the kettle on while I go and fetch the order trays through, then we can have a quick coffee before I have to deliver the supplies.'

'I think I should be coming with you as the weather's not going to let up in the next few hours and it'll surely help if I'm there with you to steady the trays as the wind could easily whip them out of your hands.'

'That's a sensible idea, but I feel awful taking up so much of your time this afternoon. I think I'll accept your offer though, as it's getting pretty wild out there and I appreciate all the help you've given me.'

'I know that, but before we load the car let's have that cup of coffee shall we, and can I butter one of those cheese scones? They smell delicious.'

'Please help yourself - there's some butter in the fridge.'

It was after three o'clock before they put the baking onto the delivery trays. Each tray was marked with the name of the shop or cafe with a list of what had to be placed into them. The lists helped Sheila organise the trays and saved time. Before leaving Muriel stacked the Aga up with more coal to keep the kitchen warm until they returned. When she opened the door she was stunned by the force of the wind and told Sheila she would bring the car as close to the house as possible. She picked up the keys, put on her shoes and a waterproof jacket.

'Grab yourself a coat of some sort Sheila, as you're certainly going to need one. I'll only be a minute or two.'

Muriel bent down by the wind and rain, went to get the car. Sheila confided in Bess, 'I don't know what we are going to do with her today Bess but don't worry, I'll make sure I stay with her until the men are safely back home.'

Muriel and Sheila put the trays as carefully as they could in the back of the car and covered them with clean tablecloths. They set off down the farm track to deliver the fresh baking to the local customers.

The wind and driving rain made the journey hazardous. The headlights were on and wipers worked at full speed; the wind was so strong it lifted the wiper blades from the windscreen and buffeted the car. Muriel knew every twist and turn of the lane and, kept as far as possible from any dangerous slopes.

'I think we should have waited a while to see if the weather might have eased off slightly but it's too late now. I can't turn back it's safer to keep going.'

'You're doing well, everything will be fine. We'll make it down safely you'll see. I'm keeping a good look out for anything and, with two pairs of eyes on the road, we'll beat the elements. Once we reach the bottom it'll be much easier.' Muriel couldn't see that Sheila had her fingers firmly crossed.

'I don't remember ever having had to drive in a storm as severe as this before, and I have driven in some weather over the years. I just pray the men are somewhere safe.'

'Let's hope so, but we really must keep positive as they will surely have made it down by now.'

Their conversation ceased and the only sounds were the car engine, the windscreen wipers, plus the wind and rain beating against the metal of the car. Muriel concentrated on the bends and kept her eye on the road through the torrential rain, until finally they reached the road below.

'Phew, that was scary to say the least,' said Muriel as she pulled the car over to a stop. 'I'll just take a breather for a few minutes before we carry on.'

Muriel rubbed her eyes, 'Just another couple of minutes to give my eyes a rest and we'll be on our way again. The sooner we get there the sooner we get back and hopefully it will have eased off by the time we come back.'

The rest of the drive was a challenge but they eventually reached their destinations with all the trays intact, and everywhere they delivered though grateful, people were surprised that Muriel had even attempted the drive in such appalling conditions. At the final drop off, the cafe owner insisted they stay and have a break, and refreshments before they set off for home.

'I'll take the empty trays to the car and lock it up. You need a rest,' Sheila said. As she put the trays into the car her mobile rang.

'Hi Mum it's Stephen, where are you? I've been trying to ring you for ages I need you to go to Muriel. There's been an accident, it's Ted.'

'Oh Stephen, what's happened?' Then without listening for the answer, she continued, 'I'm with Muriel now. She's in the cafe and I'm at her car. We're in Pooley doing her deliveries, tell me quickly what's happened?'

'Mum you must stay with her. Tell her that Ted has slipped and fall-en but try not to alarm her. Don't tell her, but he's badly hurt and uncon-scious. We daren't try to move him, but whatever you do just tell her he'll be fine and that mountain rescue are on the way. I'll keep in touch as much as I can. Dad is with him and I'm going to make my way back up to them. I'll be fine so try not to worry.'

'Take care Stephen, we don't want you having an accident as well.'

Sheila stayed in the car for several minutes. She was trembling and thinking, 'How am I going to tell her? She's been right about today all along, and this is the worst possible news to give her.' She rested her head on her arms over the steering wheel and carefully went over again and again in her head the words to break the news. She thought, 'Muriel has already spent the entire day worrying whether or not the men have actually made it safely onto the fell, and now knowing they have, I have to break this to her. It's not going to be easy.'

CHAPTER SEVENTEEN

The journey from the farm to the fell was a bumpy ride. Stephen suffered most having shared the ride with the two dogs who were excited about the day ahead and hardly sat still. When Ted finally brought the truck to a halt, he had barely pulled on the handbrake before the dogs were off and heading up the fell. Tess was ahead of Meg and didn't look back until she heard Ted's whistle. She stopped immediately, turned and ran back to him. Meg had also turned and was racing back to the men where they awaited Ted's instructions.

'Hold it Tess you're over keen this morning,' Ted said while they collected crooks and lunch boxes from the back of the truck, ready for the trek ahead. 'I hope the sheep are on their best behaviour. We need to get them down as quickly as possible and, with a bit of luck, they'll have already flocked together for shelter.'

Stephen was his usual quiet self and Ted wondered how the lad felt about his first full day shepherding, without having the added risk of a storm brewing. Low cloud and mist were already obscuring the tops and, as the morning breeze increased, he asked, 'How are you feeling Stephen? Do you reckon you are up for this?'

'Of course I am. It'll be a challenge with the weather threatening to take a turn for the worse but it's just made me more determined than ever. I can feel the adrenaline kicking in, but that's to be expected. You agree Dad?'

'It'll be doing that alright. But you know you can't beat a tough challenge to turn a boy into a man.'

'Aye you're right there Mark. I reckon we'll have him toughened up before the end of the day and by this time next year he'll be taking charge of the job.' Ted tried to remain positive but he was concerned about the weather. 'Right lads, let's get cracking. If we are going to beat the elements we need to be stepping things up a bit.'

The men knew that a shepherd's work on the fells was no easy task. The uneven terrain made for difficult walking and with sheep scattered over a large area it took time and patience searching and shepherding, until they were all gathered and could be brought down.

'We're going to have to tread carefully with the ground already wet and that's before the rain arrives and starts pouring off the tops,' said Ted. 'Stephen I need you to stay close by your father especially when we separate on the higher ground. I'll be going off ahead with Tess while you help your father, and as the sheep head down, Meg will have started herding them towards the large enclosure and hopefully you should manage to get them all in. I'll stay a little behind with Tess watching for any that try to escape, then once you've got them in fasten the gate, and start gathering those on the middle of the fell and put them in the nearest enclosure.'

They worked hard that morning with the sheep causing the men and dogs to back track several times. One ewe seemed to have been startled by something and escaped. Ted decided to leave her for the moment, fearing the whole group split up and tried to follow her. They battled an increasing wind and by half past eleven they had gathered little more than half of the sheep and were tired. Ted suggested they eat before the rain arrived. They sheltered behind the stone enclosure and took a rest. Finding a fairly comfortable though damp place to sit, they opened their bait bags with Tess and Meg next to them patiently hoping for a treat.

'How you feeling now then Stephen?'

'Great it's been hard work but I'm enjoying it. I thought the wind was going to blow me over a couple of times but I kept my balance.' He hadn't got the words out of his mouth when he had to leap to his feet to retrieve a couple of plastic bags which were about to take off in the wind. He grasped them firmly and gasped, 'Phew that was lucky, we can't have those things blowing across the fells.'

'Too true, the wind is the cause of that ewe running off, something must have scared it for it to take flight. I'll go back with Tess because I know we'll find a few more up there that have been sheltering. I could well do without it especially on a day like this but it has to be done.'

Ted was about to finish his drink when the rain arrived. 'Here it comes. I knew it wasn't far off so we had best get moving. I'll head back up with Tess for the ewe. She may not have gone too far and I'll check for strays. If you two cover the middle of the fell with Meg and herd them into the other enclosure then, when we meet back here, if all goes well between the three of us and the two dogs we'll manage to drive them all down. It'll take me a while against this wind but with a bit of luck we should be on our way down again in less than an hour. Make sure you stick together; I don't want anyone taking risks. It's too dangerous in these conditions.'

'We will. Don't worry everything will be fine, and you take your time. There's no point trying to rush, it's slippery underfoot.'

'Alright lads. Come on Tess we've work to do. Let's go and see what might still up there.' Ted knew it was not going to be easy with the weather, and he was concerned for Mark and Stephen but, having got this far, the job would be best finished as the weather was expected to last another few days. Tess was one of Ted's favourite dogs, and watching her as she ran on ahead, he smiled to himself knowing she would do the job perfectly. She was well trained and her skills were rated highly among the local farmers. When she found a stray, often hidden in the bracken, she would not give in until she had herded it with the others.

The sky had darkened. It was so dark it was as if night had arrived early. Ted knew it was going to turn into quite a storm, and with the wind increasing, it was taking him all his energy to climb and stay upright but he would not give up. Tess was nowhere to be seen which meant she would be working and had probably found the ewe. After several unsuccessful attempts to reach a spot where he could get some shelter from the wind, he decided to sit where he was for several minutes to take a breather. He wondered how Mark and Stephen were managing and prayed silently for their safe keeping. He thought about Muriel and hoped she would not be worrying too much about them, knowing well how anxious she would be. He tried to remember another day when the weather had changed so quickly while bringing the sheep down. He had faced bad conditions shepherding on the fells over the years but today was turning out to be one of the worst. He thought to himself, 'If we get them into the enclosures then I may have to think again about taking them all the way down today. For safety's sake, we'll possibly have to leave them penned until tomorrow.'

He struggled to get back to his feet and set off to find Tess when a couple of yards higher up he spotted the sheep. He whistled for Tess several times but she didn't appear. He guessed she had found another stray and started out over the rocky terrain to find her. He found it difficult to see where he was stepping with the rain lashing in his face and suddenly lost his footing, and fell hitting his head on a jagged rock.

Mark and Stephen battled against the worsening weather but were slowly managing to gather the sheep with Meg's help. Mark decided it would be safer if they herded them, as Ted said, into the nearest enclosure as the darkening sky made it difficult to see clearly. 'I wonder how Ted's managing on his own - it certainly won't be easy for him,' he shouted to Stephen, as he paused to catch his breath. 'I'd think he'd be well on his way down by now.'

The wind howled and whistled, making it hard to hear. Stephen shouted, 'Let's hope so. It's bad enough down here so I can't imagine what it must be like higher up.'

'He's done this many a time and knows the fell pretty well. He's tough is Ted. He'll manage, you'll see.'

It took longer than expected to pen the second flock. They returned to the large enclosure where they were sure to find Ted. They were worried when they saw he was not there. Mark whistled for him, but Ted didn't respond. The sound of the howling wind was all he heard but he persisted expecting he would hear Ted's whistle. Father and son looked anxiously at one another and Mark suggested, 'We'll try to get some shelter behind the enclosure wall while we wait. He's bound to be here soon. I bet Tess has found a couple of strays and that's what's delaying them. I'll carry on whistling and surely he will hear it sooner or later.'

They sat down to rest on the saturated ground to get a break from the storm. The rain was continuous and the force of the wind driving it into their faces was relentless. They decided to sit it out until Ted returned. Mark continued to whistle while Stephen scanned the horizon as far as he could see through the rain. After an hour sitting in the cold and damp there was still no sign of Ted or Tess. They feared the worst.

'Do you think we should start looking for him?'

'We don't have a choice. We have to try. We'll see what we can do but we are going to have to be careful. If we don't make contact with him soon then we'll have to go down and call mountain rescue.'

Suddenly Stephen shouted, 'Dad, Dad, it's Tess!' Tess ran towards them and circled around over and over again, jumping and barking. They knew she was trying to tell them something and decided to follow her. Stephen checked the gate was fastened securely so the sheep would not get out. It was obvious Tess would lead them to Ted so at least they wouldn't have to search, but Mark was worried what they would find. The two dogs ran ahead and then back down, making sure the men were following until at last they found Ted. They were shocked to find him lying unconscious with a broken leg as they could see it was twisted badly underneath him. 'Quick Stephen, you have to get back down the fell and call mountain rescue urgently.'

Before heading off, Mark kept talking to Ted but there was no response he felt for his pulse and thankfully it was there. He ran his hands gently over his head to feel for any bleeding and was pleased to find nothing.

'I'll have to stay here with Ted, and hope he starts to come round. I can't leave him. Take Meg with you Stephen. I'm sorry, I don't like asking you to go alone but there's nothing else we can do if we're all to get off the fell alive.'

'I'll manage don't worry. Come on Meg let's be off. Let's not waste any time.' Stephen left the older men and made his way down the fell with Meg at his side. He knew he wouldn't get mobile reception on the fell so continued down until he reached a house where the shocked residents showed him their phone. He trembled as he called 999 and waited. A voice asked, 'Emergency, which service do you require?'

'Police, there's been an accident on the fell.'

'Where are you calling from?'

'Beda Fell House. It's Ted Thornton the farmer, he's unconscious. My father's with him. We were bringing the sheep down when...' The voice on the other end interrupted.

'Alright, how many of you are there?'

'Three - Ted, my father and I. It's Ted who's injured.'

'Give me the number of the phone you are ringing from.' Stephen repeated the number twice to make sure she had heard him correctly.

The police receptionist said, 'The mountain rescue team will be there as soon as they can. Try to keep calm.'

'I will, thanks.' The mountain rescue team soon rang and he told them where he was and roughly where Ted had fallen. He was pleased to hear they were already on their way.

'Stay where you are and we'll be with you as quick as we can. You'll be able to help guide us.'

He patted Meg and confided, 'I don't think it will take them too long to reach us Meg, and hopefully Dad will have been able to help Ted until they get to him. I'll ask the people here if I can ring Mum so she can go over to tell Muriel what has happened and stay with her until we return.'

Four members of Patterdale Mountain Rescue Team had set out immediately they received the call. The journey in good weather took around 40 minutes, but in severe conditions it would take longer though they knew exactly where they were heading. Stephen waited patiently with Meg while the couple in the house put a cup of hot sweet tea in his hands. His thoughts were with the men up on the fell and he talked to Meg, 'I hope they're both alright, lass especially Ted, as he looked to be in a bad way.' He got no reaction from the dog, but having Meg near him he felt better while he waited for the rescue team to arrive. After what seemed a long time he could just make out through the window, the faint blue light of the ambulance making its way up the fell. Relieved he knew it was the rescue team and several minutes later the phone rang.

'Hello, is that mountain rescue?' Stephen's voice sounded optimistic.

'Yes we're not too far from you now. How are you?'

'Apart from feeling worried, I'm fine. It's just nice to hear your voice and know that you're not so far away.'

'I trust you are still where you said we'd find you?'

'Yes, I am. It's the closest place to where Ted and my father are.'

'Good. It won't be long now until we're with you.' Stephen felt relieved that at last there was help at hand. He put his coat back on and waited at the door, thanking the couple for letting him use the telephone and for the tea. He patted Meg who rested her head against his leg, as though reassuring him all would be well.

'They're on their way now Meg but, before we leave here, I think I should let Mum and Muriel know what's happening.' He continued talking to her as though she were a person, about to agree with him whilst waiting for his mother to answer.

'Stephen at last what's happening?'

'Don't panic, they're nearly here. How are you and how has Muriel taken the news?'

'She's very worried as you would expect. We're still at the café where we heard the mountain rescue going through and hoped it was in answer to your call. Have you any idea how Ted and your Dad are?'

'I've no idea I'm still at Beda Fell House. It's really bad here and it's getting worse. I've had to wait here for the mountain rescue team to lead them up the fell. They'll be here very soon so try not to worry.' He could hear his mother's voice panicking.

'It's alright Mum - now listen to me. I think it would be better if you and Muriel got back to the cottage or the farm. I see no sense in you sitting in the café when we don't know where they'll take Ted once they reach him. It may be that he can be taken home but they might take him to hospital.' He paused before continuing, 'Also Mum you really need to look in on Tia to see if she's alright, as she's nearly sure to have had her pups by now. They'll need checking to make sure they're all feeding properly, so I think you should both go home.'

'Alright, I'll ask Muriel and see what she wants to do. Be careful, and we'll see you when you get back home.'

'You will, bye Mum.' He heard the Land Rover engine revving in the distance as it made its way up the track. He went outside and the vehicle arrived. Four men wearing bright red waterproof jackets jumped out and set about getting items of rescue equipment ready to head off on foot up the fell. They were pleased to find him looking well and gave him a waterproof to wear before they set off with Stephen leading the way.

Further up the fell Tess heard the men and ran down to meet them almost as though she knew they were there to help. When Mark saw the red clad volunteers approaching he admired their dedication, courage, and skill. He told Ted, 'Everything will be fine Ted, help is here.' Whether Ted heard him or not he didn't know but he felt he was reassuring him.

'How are you?' they asked almost in unison when they were within hearing distance.

'I'm not bad considering it's been so rough here today, but I'm very concerned about Ted. I've been talking to him hoping it might bring him round but nothing, and I've kept checking his pulse which seems to be fairly regular. I haven't attempted to move him as you can see his leg looks badly trapped beneath him.'

'We found you quickly as Stephen led us straight here. Dave here will give you a check over to make sure you're in decent shape, while Bob, Pete and I take a look at Ted,' said Mike.

Ted was in a far worse condition than Mark had even dared to imagine and the paramedics decided that he was too badly injured to be stretchered off the fell. His concussion caused concern, and they suspected spinal injuries as well as a broken leg. They decided to radio for the air ambulance helicopter, if it could fly in the conditions, as Ted needed urgent hospital treatment.

Mark was upset that Ted was in such a bad way and asked Stephen to go back down to Beda Fell House to warn his mother and Muriel, that the rescue helicopter had been called to take him to hospital. Mike said: 'You're not going down there again on your own Stephen.' Knowing the rest could manage without him, he set off with Stephen and Meg ahead of the others. They headed for the mountain rescue ambulance below.

✄ ✄ ✄

Sheila persuaded Muriel they should go home, and suggested she drove. They had just arrived when Stephen rang, to find out where they were.

'Oh Stephen, we've just got home. What's happening? I am so worried. How bad is Ted you must tell me?'

'From what the mountain rescue have told us he definitely has a broken leg and they are concerned there may be other injuries. They said it would be dangerous to carry him down so they have radioed for a helicopter to airlift him to hospital.'

'He is going to be alright isn't he?' asked Sheila.

'I'm sure he will be,' Stephen said. 'Don't worry we'll be heading home as soon as Ted is on his way to hospital and Dad will be able to tell you more.'

'Thanks we'll see you soon.' The telephone call eased her mind and she suggested they should pop over to see if Tia had had her pups.

Muriel's thoughts were with Ted and how badly injured he must be if they had to call a helicopter. As they reached the door of the cottage they heard the whirring of the helicopter propellers above the roar of the wind. They hugged each other and listened as it flew towards the fell. Sheila said, 'It's far better he gets to hospital as quickly as possible.'

'I know you're right, but I'm finding it hard to take in. You know how much Ted means to me. He's been my rock through so much and for so many years that the thought of losing him is beyond words...'

'Stop talking like that. He has a broken leg and the reason they'll have called the air ambulance is because it's too difficult for him to be stretchered down on foot in this weather. You have to agree it's better he is checked over thoroughly while he's in hospital, then they can send him home as soon as he has the all clear. Now let's get the kettle on. If you see to the kettle, I'll stoke the fire so that you can get warm, then I'll pop outside and take a look at Tia while I still have my coat on.'

She went out to the shed where Tia had been left warm and comfortable to deliver her pups and, for the first time that day she felt some excitement. As she opened the door she saw lying on the straw wagging her tail Tia with five pups. She checked them to make sure they were warm and had fed. The smallest one was struggling, so she carefully helped her onto a teat and waited until she was suckling properly, before running back to the cottage with the good news.

'Oh that's wonderful. I must go over and see them straight away,' said Muriel. She pulled on her coat and they went to look at the five new arrivals. For the first time that day Muriel had something to feel happy about. 'You must let Stephen know as soon as he's back. He'll be so thrilled and it will help lift his spirits knowing Tia is fine and all the pups are well.'

'I will, but I must feed Tia before I do anything else.'

Stephen had left everything prepared for Tia, and Sheila just had to check that all was well. She went to the house to get some warm milk for Tia, and looked back as she went out of the door to see Muriel gently stroking the pups. They helped take her mind off the worry and pain she was feeling about Ted. Sheila gave Tia the milk and then they left her to rest with her litter.

CHAPTER EIGHTEEN

The storm raged on. The biting wind and heavy rain made work difficult for the doctor and paramedics. The team struggled under the extreme conditions to stabilise Ted's injuries ready for him to be transported. Tess was more and more unsettled as she tried to return to Ted's side where she had waited patiently and it took Mark all his time to settle her, so the medics could attend to him. When the doctor finished the examination he said to Mark, 'We need to take him to the Cumberland Infirmary where we'll hand him over to the trauma team who will be waiting for us as soon as we arrive. Will you be coming along with us?' Mark hesitated - he was torn where his loyalties lay - it was a difficult choice but, after thinking he shook his head.

'I know I'll be leaving Ted in excellent hands so I've decided to go down with the mountain rescue. That way I can be with Tess, poor thing. She won't want to leave unless she's with someone she knows. The minute you start lifting Ted towards the helicopter I know she'll try to follow you but, even more importantly, I think I should see Muriel to explain what's happened.'

The doctor agreed with Mark and assured him, 'I understand. You know he will be well looked after and we'll have reached the hospital before you're even back at the farm. Will you ask his wife to ring the hospital as soon as she can, as they'll want some information from her.'

Mark leaned towards Ted, tapped him gently on the shoulder and hoped he could hear him, 'You're in good hands Ted. They'll soon have you fixed and back home safely. Don't worry about the sheep or Tess - we'll take care of that.'

The helicopter crew were anxious to get away before the weather deteriorated any further. Mark said, 'I'll see that Muriel rings as soon as possible. Thank you for everything.' Ted, was strapped onto a stretcher, and the team transferred him to the helicopter. Mark watched nervously and waited until he could see Ted being lifted on board and the doors secured for take off. The helicopter propellers increased speed rapidly, the noise was deafening, even above the sound of the wind, as the aircraft tilted and swerved off the fell in a northerly direction.

Tess had tried to follow Ted, but Mark hung on to her collar and, along with the mountain rescue team, they began to make their way slowly back down to the waiting ambulance, where Stephen and Mike were waiting with Meg. Now warmer and drier Meg spotted Tess and raced towards her and they greeted each other like long lost friends. Likewise father and son greeted each other as though they had been parted for years. Stephen suggested, 'I'll take the dogs down. I think you should go in the ambulance to the road and then we'll manage the rest of the way over the fields to the truck together.'

Before Mark had time to answer, Mike said, 'I'll come with you Stephen. Mark you need to go down in the ambulance because you've been out in this weather for long enough today and you've had a lot of stress. We need to make sure you're well enough to drive back to the farm before we leave. I know you say you're alright, but we need to be certain. Dave will drive slowly so that he has us in his sight until we reach the road.'

Mark had no choice and agreed. Stephen and Mike followed with the dogs to meet on the road below. The team were satisfied that the two men were well and said a farewell as another call was coming in on the radio. Mark and Stephen made the rest of the journey back to the truck on foot. The ambulance raced off and as it did so Stephen remarked on the wonderful job they had done.

Tess and Meg were already on the way across the field. They knew their day's work was over and that they would ride in the truck back to the farm. It took the men longer than usual to cross the field, taking what seemed like one step forward and two back, as they headed into the wind and rain. The dogs came back as if to guide them and they eventually arrived at the truck which had been left with the key in the ignition. They climbed in grateful for the shelter of the vehicle, and with the engine running, they started to warm up. Mark said, 'It's time to head back for a few home comforts. I only wish we didn't have to take bad news with us but it has to be done, and the sooner we tell them the better. I can imagine what kind of a state Muriel will have been in since you broke the news.'

'Me too, and I imagine Mam will have had a difficult time trying to console her, but we'll soon be home and that will make things easier for them knowing we are back safe and there to help.' Once back at the farm they went to the cottage where they knew the women would be waiting.

'Oh quick tell me is Ted going to be alright? Are you both okay? I can't thank you enough for helping and we are relieved to have you home safe.' Muriel said, barely stopping to take a breath. Mark took her by the arm and guided her in the direction of the open door. 'Let's go inside where it's warm and we can all sit down and we'll tell you everything that's happened since we left this morning.' He tried not to hurt her feelings as he knew how much she needed to know, but he also wanted to see his wife and get warmed up.

'Of course, I'm sorry,' Muriel stepped aside to let them enter the cottage. Sheila was relieved they were home, and was waiting to welcome her husband and son. She hugged them both, her eyes moist and said, 'Oh thank goodness you're here. What a terrible day it's been. You need to get out of your wet clothes and into something dry and then come and warm yourselves by the fire. I'll have a hot drink ready for you and there's a casserole in the oven as soon as you are both warm.'

'I'm going over to see Tia and the pups before I get changed and settle down,' Stephen said as he was keen to see the new arrivals. Muriel said she would go too, despite being desperate to hear about Ted, to let Mark and Sheila have time to sort themselves out. As they crossed the yard she said, 'The pups are beautiful Stephen, and Tia is already turning out to be a wonderful mother.'

When he saw the pups he soon forgot about everything that had happened and knelt down to stroke Tia and then picked up her pups one by one to check they were all healthy. The arrival of the pups had eased some of the pain and stress. As they walked back to the cottage Muriel's thoughts were with Ted and she said, 'I'll ring the hospital now and find out how Ted is and then I'll have to travel up to Carlisle tonight to see him. I'll have to ring his parents too.'

Stephen didn't answer but thought, 'How can she possibly make the journey tonight? It would be far too risky and besides there are animals to feed and jobs still to be done at the farm before it gets too late.' He kept his thoughts to himself knowing all four would be discussing what had happened on the fell and what they would need to do to make sure everything was cared for. Back inside, Muriel disappeared to make her call and Stephen changed into dry clothes.

A hot drink was waiting in no time and father and son sat by the fire which Sheila had stacked with coal and logs to warm the sitting room. Leaning towards the fire their hands almost touching the burning coal, Mark and Stephen began to relax for the first time that day. Mark said, 'That was a lovely cup of tea. I don't think I've enjoyed one so much in a long time.'

Sheila smiled, 'I can see that. It's nice to see you both with a bit of colour in your cheeks again. When Muriel has finished her call I'll set the table and we can eat. I'm worried that she will want to go to the hospital tonight. I can't see the weather easing and I don't think the hospital will be ready for Ted to have visitors.'

Stephen warned, 'She's already told me she plans to go to the hospital tonight and those were exactly my thoughts when she mentioned it.'

'Well all we can do is discuss it and hopefully we can agree what is the best thing to do.' Mark had barely spoken these words when Muriel entered the room looking very pale and apprehensive. Everything went quiet and no one said a word for a few minutes.

Finally Muriel broke the silence, 'They've told me it's not a good idea to go to the hospital tonight as Ted is in the X-ray department and will be taken into theatre very soon as his leg is broken in three places. He has managed to say a few words to them and he told them that he could not feel his legs which could mean he has spinal injuries.' She lowered her head. She desperately did not want to believe what she had been told. Her voice shook, 'If this means he'll never walk again I promise I will look after him every day no matter what it takes. He has always been my rock and now it's my turn to be his.'

Sheila said, 'Let's not start worrying too much before we have the full results Muriel. We are all here for you and anything we can do we'll be ready to help.' She crossed the room and hugged Muriel. She faced yet another crisis, and Sheila hoped she would find the strength to get through it.

'You may be right, but at this precise moment I can't do anything else but think the worst, and I think I should drive to the hospital tonight to be near him.'

Mark said, 'If they're telling you it's unwise, then I think you should take their advice and let them do their work. You should stay at home until they let you know that you can see him, then I'll travel up with you.'

'You're probably right but it's hard not being with him at the very time in his life I should be there.'

'I understand what you're saying but he won't know whether you are there or not, and if you wait until morning then hopefully the weather will have calmed and he will be well enough to see you.' Sheila and Stephen remained quiet leaving the reasoning to Mark.

Sheila said, 'I'll go to the kitchen and start organising some supper.' She glanced at Stephen and asked, 'Would you like to give me a hand?' He realised that his mother's request was not to help in the kitchen, but to leave the two together to talk and he followed her out of the room.

'I think your Dad will manage to get through to her that she can't go to the hospital tonight, but I do understand how hard it must be for her.'

'Let's get the supper on the table then we can tell you both about what happened, and remind Muriel she still has to go across to the farm to finish off jobs there. We'll feel better when we've eaten. Then we can start to work out how we can help run the farm while Ted's in hospital.'

The men explained everything that had happened on the fell and they discussed what could be done to keep the farm running as normal. Muriel accepted that she wouldn't be allowed to see Ted that night so was resigned to waiting until the morning and she knew there were jobs to be done on the farm. She was happy for Stephen to go with her the next day and for him to help run the farm. Stephen quickly gathered enough gear for the unexpected overnight stay and Muriel drove him, along with Tess and Meg back to the farm to start the evening jobs. Muriel decided to ring the hospital to find out the X-ray results and when she could visit.

When they arrived at the farm the dogs sped off across the yard to the barn where they knew they would be fed. In the kitchen Bess was still stretched in front of the Aga where Muriel stroked her, thinking how fretful she would be when she realised Ted was not at home.

'It's been a bad day Bess, and we're not going to see Ted for quite some time by the sounds of it,' her voice faded as she swallowed back the lump in her throat. Stephen stoked the Aga and Muriel went around the house putting on lights and checking the spare room where Stephen would stay. When Bess had been fed they put on dry outdoor clothes and set out to do the nightly chores. Stephen insisted they stay together to feed the dogs, lock up the hens and make sure that there was enough hay and water for the ponies and goat.

First they fed the sheepdogs. 'You've done yourselves proud lasses,' Stephen patted each dog as he fed them. 'Ted will want to know how you are when we visit him tomorrow.'

'He certainly will, and from what Mark told me about how Tess ran to warn you that something had happened, and then barely left his side until he was taken from the fell, he will be moved by her dedication, though he would never have doubted she would have stayed with him.'

'She was a star, in fact they both were. It was pretty grim up there in those conditions and they were both soaked. Alright then, dogs fed, let's get across to the field and see what's been happening there today.'

They struggled against the wind and rain to reach the field. The hens were already in the coops and were only to lock up for the night. Lady and Blaze were beside the electric fence waiting when they heard them heading towards the field and, like the dogs, were wet through. Most of the hay had been blown around the field by the wind and they had to bring a fresh bale. They went back across the yard to collect enough to fill the tractor tyres used as troughs for the ponies and a smaller tyre which held enough for Nancy the goat. There was enough water as the rain had kept the buckets topped up. Stephen took some hay for Nancy knowing Muriel was a little wary of her. The chores completed, they went back to the house to telephone about Ted.

The Aga had warmed the kitchen and Muriel offered Stephen a beer and poured herself a glass of wine before she rang the hospital where she was told Ted was still in theatre. The hospital suggested she had a good night's rest, and rang again in the morning when they would be able to give her more information about Ted's condition. Stephen could tell by her expression that they had not told her any good news and didn't ask her anything, leaving her to tell him when she was ready. After a while she said, 'He's still in theatre so they have told me not to ring again until morning. It's going to be a long night. I hope I can manage to get some sleep to help pass away the hours.'

'I guess it will be a long night, but if you have another drink it might help you sleep for a little while at least.' Minutes later the phone rang - it was Sheila to ask if they had heard anything.

'Nothing until morning Sheila. He's in theatre so I think I'm going to have an early night and I'll ring you tomorrow, as soon as I have any news, then you can let Mark know what time I'd like to leave. Thanks Sheila for everything you've done today. Goodnight and sleep well.' She refilled her glass and gave Stephen another beer, then took the kettle off the Aga to fill a hot water bottle to warm his bed. She returned to the kitchen and put away the baking that had been left to cool offering Stephen something to eat.

'No thanks Muriel I'm fine, but another beer wouldn't go amiss.'

She passed him another bottle and suggested she showed him his room before he had his beer so that she was able to get an early night.

CHAPTER NINETEEN

It proved hard for Muriel to sleep, as she hadn't slept alone since she and Ted were married. The bed felt empty so she pulled his pillows under the duvet to fill the space where he should have been and hugged them. She thought about the first time they had met when she was still a schoolgirl. On the day of his interview he was asked to stay for tea with the family so that she and Michael could meet him when they returned from school.

She remembered being fascinated by his Geordie accent which she tried to imitate when she teased him. Over the years he had lost his Geordie twang and picked up some of the Cumbrian accent but there were times when he reverted back to it, especially when he was talking to his parents. From the day he arrived at Felix Hill Farm he had become a member of the family living with them almost like a relative. Her parents told her he was always willing to help in whatever way he could and never refused to do anything that was asked. In those early days she never imagined that she would fall in love with him, marry, and spend her life running the farm with him.

Startled by a strange sound her thoughts were interrupted. She remembered Stephen was sleeping across the landing and it had most probably come from his room. She worried as she remembered that he was sleeping in the room Ted had first used when he came to live at the farm. She listened for a while to see if the noise was repeated but all was silent.

She imagined Stephen following in Ted's footsteps as he was as much a part of the family and farm, as Ted had been. She had not thought this before but realised they treated him like the son they had never had. He had visited the farm regularly with his parents ever since they moved into Felix Cottage and the two families had grown close. Would he, she wondered, take over the role of running the farm in Ted's place if his injuries turned out more serious than first thought?

Ted was at that time 55 and, if he could no longer do as much as he used to, she knew Stephen would learn from him and take charge. The thought of Ted never being able to work again horrified her and she pushed it to the back of her mind, but no matter how hard she tried it would not go away. Her only consolation was that, if this was the case, she would be happy if Stephen were the one to step into Ted's shoes. She eventually fell asleep before the sound of Stephen crossing the landing on his way to the bathroom woke her. She turned to the clock and was pleased to see it was almost 6am. She jumped out of bed washed, dressed and was downstairs before Stephen had time to return to his room. For once she ignored Bess, as first and foremost she wanted news of Ted and she rang the hospital.

The ward sister said, 'Your husband is very poorly Mrs Thornton and has been transferred by helicopter to the Spinal Unit at Royal Victoria Infirmary in Newcastle. We tried to make contact with you earlier but couldn't get an answer. We knew you were ringing before leaving home. Ted managed to talk a little, but all he could remember was that he was on the fell in bad weather. He couldn't remember the accident but he is getting the best care possible. You can ring the RVI as they'll be able to update you on his condition.'

'He is going to be alright isn't he?' Muriel asked.

'He will be alright, but we believe he's facing a long time in hospital while he gets well.'

'Oh dear, it doesn't sound good. Thank you for everything. I'll go over to Newcastle later today to see him.' She had just put the telephone down when the kitchen door opened and Stephen came in and asked, 'What's the news from the hospital?'

'Not very good news I'm afraid. They have transferred him to the RVI in Newcastle with suspected spinal injuries. The good news is he's been talking a little so there are no serious head injuries though he doesn't remember anything about the accident.' Muriel was silent, as she tried to remember everything the nurse had said.

'Oh that doesn't sound very good. I think I should ring Mum and Dad to break the news. But first I'll get the Aga warmed up and feed Bess.'

Muriel realised she had completely ignored Bess and went over to give her a pat. Bess sensed something was wrong.

'Thanks Stephen. I'll put the kettle on and cook us some breakfast.' Muriel always thought of food first and didn't want anyone to go hungry.

'Thanks. I certainly won't say no to some breakfast but, after that you just forget about everything else and I'll see to the farm.'

Stephen rang his parents, 'Hi Mum, just to let you know that Muriel rang the hospital and they said Ted has been transferred to the RVI in Newcastle. They're concerned about his spine but I'll leave it to Muriel to explain everything to you. She plans to go over to Newcastle to visit him today. What plans have you and Dad made for today?'

'Well we spent much of last night weighing everything up and have decided that I should go to the hospital with Muriel. Of course, last night we expected it would be Carlisle. Dad says that you two need to finish the job of fetching the ewes down as soon as possible. So I've already rung work to explain that I'm needed here. They were only too pleased to allow as much time as I want in the circumstances.'

'Oh that's good of them. Is Dad there? Can I speak to him?'

'No he's over checking Tia and the pups but he'll be back any minute and I'll get him to ring straight away.'

Five minutes later the phone rang, Muriel left it for Stephen to answer guessing who it was.

'How are things?' asked Mark.

'As well as can be expected considering the news. We're just going to have breakfast and then Muriel plans to head over to the hospital. Mum tells me she's going with her. I haven't even looked outside yet today - what's the weather like?'

'It's still raining, but the wind has dropped so it will be much easier up on the fell. Travelling across to Newcastle will be much easier today.'

'That's good news. How are Tia and the pups this morning?'

'They're all fine, so nothing to worry about there. I'll come over in the car this morning and bring your Mum with me, as it will be better if they go in Muriel's car. We'll head back up the fell as soon we can and get the sheep down. It shouldn't take too long today. I might go up and look for the stray. We'll be able to count up today and see if any others are missing.'

'If you do we go together. We don't want a repeat of yesterday... I'll see you when you get here.'

'How are they over at the cottage?' Muriel asked before Stephen had even put the phone down.

'They're fine. Tia and the pups are great, Mum is going to the hospital with you instead of Dad as he says it's important that we get the sheep off the fell today. So you need not be worrying about anything, just eat your breakfast and get ready to head off.'

'You are kind. I don't know how I'd manage without you.'

'Don't even think about it. Now, let's have breakfast.' He smiled as he sat down at the table and poured the tea.

'That looks and smells good,' said Stephen, as he added tomato ketchup to his fried breakfast, and buttered some thick slices of bread.

'You eat as much as you can. It's going to be another cold day on the fell. At least your mother and I will be warm in the car, though I have to say I know where I would rather be going. Poor Ted, I can't believe this has happened. As soon as I find out exactly how he is and what will be happening I'll need to let his parents know.' She thought for a few moments as she pushed her food round the plate. The strain of the last 24 hours had finally sunk in and she felt very tired. 'Do you think I should let Ted's parents know before I have been to see him? I do feel for them as they are elderly now, and I don't want to upset them with bad news. But, when it's about Ted I have to let them know. I'm rather worried that they will take it badly, but at least he's not too far away from them now.'

Stephen did not reply. He thought he ought to help Muriel, but this decision was one that he thought his parents could help with.

'Wait until Mum and Dad arrive. It'll be better if they help you make that decision as I'm not sure what would be the best thing to do.'

'You're probably right. It's silly of me to be asking you such questions. After all you have plenty of other things on your mind, helping with everything on the farm and the animals to feed.'

Bess's ears pricked up as she heard a car heading up the track. Muriel went to meet Mark and Sheila at the door.

'Morning, how are you?' Mark asked in a friendly tone.

Muriel stood aside to let them into the house and replied, 'Very worried as you'd expect. I'll feel better once I've seen him. It must be pretty serious for them to transfer him to Newcastle but, until I have spoken to a doctor and heard the full extent of his injuries, I don't really know what to think. It has been a comfort having Stephen stay last night, knowing there was someone else in the house.'

'You know he can stay here as long as it takes. After all we are near enough to see him every day and make sure he's managing alright. I'll be here most days when I'm not expected to be working somewhere else.' Mark hoped to reassure Muriel she would not be left to cope alone.

'Let's get going shall we?' Sheila was concerned that they had a much longer journey to make than first thought. 'I'll tidy up in here while you get ready Muriel, if that's alright?'

'Are you sure you can spare the time to travel to Newcastle with me? What if we can't make it back again today for some reason?'

'Stop worrying Muriel. We'll face the challenges one at a time - just get yourself ready.'

Stephen remembered the cats, Misty and Smokey, had not been fed so put some food out for them and told his father, 'I'm going over the yard to feed the dogs. After that I'll let the hens out and feed them, then I'll see to the others in the field before we set off. The eggs can be left until we get back as the most important job for us today is to bring those ewes down.' He sounded confident and his father felt proud of him. He thought Stephen was handling the situation calmly and professionally so he would leave him to take the lead and only help if there was a problem.

'You're right. While you're over at the field I'll go and put what we need into the truck and get the dogs in the back as soon as they have finished eating. I'm sure you ladies have lots to do so we'll say our good-byes for now. Make sure you ring here and leave a message on the answerphone as soon as your reach the hospital to let us know that you've arrived safely.'

'We will as soon as we have parked. Don't forget we've never been to the RVI before so it may take us some time to find it,' said Sheila. Muriel had gone upstairs to get ready while Sheila tidied the kitchen.

Mark picked up a set of house keys and the keys for the truck . He and Stephen left determined to bring the Herdwick ewes down to the in-bye land. They wanted to make sure that in a few months time they would have the pleasure of watching Ted smiling, as he admired the new born lambs skipping in next spring's sunshine.

Chapter Twenty

The weather improved as the November storms gave way to more settled conditions. There was a slight covering of snow on the tops of the fells, but temperatures were slightly above average for the time of the year. Stephen and Mark returned the ewes to the fells just before Christmas where they stayed until April when they were brought down to fields near the farm for lambing.

Ted stayed in the Royal Victoria Infirmary in Newcastle. Muriel with people to help, worked on the farm, looked after the house and cottage, and made daily visits to the hospital. Ted's injuries were serious, so they had a rota to take it in turns to visit him, while always having someone at the farm. Muriel managed her usual work around the house and farm. Mark and Sheila chose Friday as their day off from their usual work to visit Ted and enjoy some time to themselves. Financially they could not survive without a regular income, and they both continued to fit their work in around Muriel and the farm.

Mark, Sheila, Stephen and Muriel worked as a team. They worked hard, shared laughter and tears, and most important they were always there to pick each other up when needed. The one thing they hadn't expected to be a problem was Tess. She fretted for Ted and every time a vehicle headed up the track she seemed to think it was him returning. They discussed locking her inside with Bess but knew she wouldn't be happy. Tess had never been a house dog, and they understood how she missed Ted. She was allowed some freedom in the farmyard, as she had been used to this since a pup. Whenever a vehicle approached they had to keep an eye out for her.

The festive season arrived and it was quiet at the farm. Muriel did not want celebrations until Ted returned home and spent Christmas day at the cottage after she and Mark returned from a visit to the hospital. Ted had tried to stop them from visiting that day, but Muriel insisted she could not bear the thought of Christmas without seeing him.

The New Year brought some good news. The hospital said that Ted could be transferred back to the Cumberland Infirmary before the end of January. He would stay there for treatment, including occupational therapy to help him walk again. This news came as a relief and gave them time to reschedule their work in time for Ted's move back to Cumbria.

Muriel planned a new visiting rota and suggested to her friends, 'Only one of us will need to visit at a time now, as he's so much nearer home. You know how grateful I am to you all for everything you've done, so don't feel bad about it if you don't have time to visit.'

Sheila quickly replied, 'Now you know that we will all make time to visit. Ted's recovery means as much to us as it does to you and we'll not stop helping until he's back fit and well and running the farm again.'

'Hear, hear,' agreed Stephen. He seemed to have grown up quickly over the past couple of months. They had told Ted how well he managed the farm and Ted was delighted and told Muriel that he could be a future right hand man.

'Together we will teach him everything he needs to know about running the farm successfully for us when we're not able to do it ourselves,' he told Muriel. He knew that Stephen's heart was in farming and that he would never leave his Cumbria. Although she felt these words were a little premature considering their age, she didn't question him knowing he would remain true to his word and that Stephen would never leave the area.

Muriel felt it was a relief to have Sheila, Mark and Stephen's continued support when Ted was transferred back to Carlisle. She knew Ted's return to Cumbria did not mean an early return to the farm, and that there would be many weeks, even months, before he could come home and get back to work.

'I don't know how I'll ever be able to repay you for everything you've done for Ted and I over these past couple of months.' Muriel thought the family were lovely and she was concerned to let them know how much their help meant.

Mark said, 'Repayment is not a word in our vocabulary because we know that, had the shoe been on the other foot, you would have done exactly the same for us. So please forget about it and together we'll complete the new rota before Stephen and I have to head back over to finish at the farm for today.'

The days following the accident passed with barely a hitch. Sheila insisted she cooked an evening meal for Muriel each day at the cottage to make sure she was eating well. Stephen continued to sleep and work at the farm and only visited his parent's home for supper, and to take his dirty washing. He also went home to see Tia and her pup Cass the one he had chosen to keep. Reluctantly he had sold the other four.

At the end of January Ted was transferred by ambulance back to the Cumberland Infirmary. Muriel and Stephen were there to welcome him when he finally arrived and was transferred to the ward. They watched nervously as he was lifted gently onto the bed and realised for the first time how serious his injuries were. They had never seen him being moved during visits and it was a shock to see how many staff were needed to move him without inflicting further injury. Once comfortably settled, the nursing staff left them to it and Muriel leaned over and gave him a hug saying how pleased she was to have him nearer home.

'Having you back in Cumbria is a step nearer to home and we're all waiting for the day that you return to the farm.'

'Me too,' he replied. 'Nice to see you Stephen and I've been hearing you are now so experienced on the farm I may not have a job to come home to.'

'I don't think so Ted! I certainly had to learn quickly but without Muriel and Dad I could never have done it. You just concentrate on getting mobile again because I'm looking forward to us working together again, very soon I hope.'

'Aye you're right lad. I need to get back on my feet again as soon as possible. I can't tell you how hard it has been lying here day after day. I know you have all visited but you know, you miss the sheep and, as for the dogs, well it goes without saying. I just long to be home to see them again, though I understand Tess has become a bit of a problem?'

'She has, but nothing we can't handle. We just need to look out for her when vehicles are coming. It's natural that she's reacting that way and is missing you, after all she stayed with you the entire time of the accident,' said Stephen.

Muriel agreed, 'She'll be fine. I can't imagine what she'll be like the day you do come home. We'll need to fasten her up until you are safely inside the house.'

'I think you're right. But that day looks to be a while off yet.'

Ted raised his eyebrows at Stephen, 'Don't you be too sure lad. I'm doing my best to get fit as quickly as possible, and I can't wait to cuddle Muriel again.'

Muriel looked slightly embarrassed by his remarks, but agreed, 'Me too, but it might be a while yet.'

'Anything worth having is worth waiting for, and that day will come sooner than you imagine.'

Muriel had her doubts but remained silent. They stayed with him for around an hour before they were asked to leave. Stephen had noticed an attractive nurse working on Ted's ward and hoped she would be working her shifts during his future visits.

Mark covered for them at the farm that day, knowing that things would be easier with the travelling time to hospital drastically reduced. They hoped Ted would make it home before lambing season but no-one had forecast a possible date.

The visiting rota worked out well with few changes - except they noticed Stephen was asking to join Muriel on one or two of her visits. Neither Muriel or his parents suspected anything but Ted noticed that the attractive nurse was more often than not working when Stephen visited. He would find some trivial reason for her to have to attend to him and then began pulling her leg about it but she remained professional. One night before leaving the hospital Stephen followed her out of the ward using the excuse that he wanted Muriel and Ted to have some time alone.

'I know what he's up to Muriel. He has a shine for that young nurse. You mark my words, I've been watching them over the weeks and I can tell the feeling is mutual. Mind you she's a bonny lass and a very good nurse.'

'Are you sure about that Ted? Don't you spread rumours that might not be true.'

'Watch this space,' he said laughing. 'I'll not be seeing the last of her when I leave this hospital.'

Meanwhile Stephen and the nurse were exchanging phone numbers. As Stephen wote down her name he asked, 'I don't think Nurse Johnson sounds quite the name I want in my contacts list.' Smiling she said, 'Zoe's my first name, Zoe Johnson. Of course I don't have to ask you what yours is as Ted keeps talking to me about you whenever he has the chance.'

'Oh is that right? I'll have to have words with him.'

'I'd rather you didn't because he could tell that we like each other and has been scheming to try to arrange for us to meet some time.'

'He's a dark horse - so that's what he gets up to in here is it?'

'I'm not complaining are you?'

'I can't say I am.'

Muriel appeared from the ward, Zoe made a sharp exit into one of the side rooms, and Stephen popped back to say goodbye to Ted whose grin stretched from ear to ear. He said, 'She's a beauty. You ask her out you know you want to and so does she.'

Stephen shook his head in amusement and turned away smiling, 'Bye Ted we'll see. Just you keep up the good work - that's getting back on your feet not playing matchmaker between nurses and visitors.' At the same time Stephen hoped Ted was right about Zoe and that when he rang her later she would be pleased. He thought, 'Time will tell no doubt, but it certainly won't be for the want of me trying. I'll try my hardest to arrange to take her out sometime.' He had a quick look to see if he could see Zoe as he left the ward, but she had vanished and he walked quickly to catch up with Muriel.

CHAPTER TWENTY ONE

Winter turned to spring with no news of Ted returning home and he watched his favourite season sadly from his hospital bed. When the spring sun shone through the window it was hard to appreciate the time of year, as he was unable to hear birds singing, the first cuckoo, or to see spring flowers pushing their way through the warm soil, or the new shoots on the trees, soon to produce an abundance of colour to last throughout the summer. He found this disheartening, but hardest of all was the thought he would not be at the farm for lambing to see the new lambs skipping around in the warm sunshine. It was difficult to keep optimistic - he said he had been in hospital long enough and he could manage at home. In his heart he knew he couldn't return until he was able to stand unaided and to walk short distances alone. This did not stop him pestering the doctors about going home.

The one thing that lifted his spirits was the blossoming romance between Stephen and Zoe. Not only was Ted delighted for them but Mark and Sheila, along with Zoe's parents and Muriel, were happy to watch their relationship grow. Zoe had visited the farm on her days off and would get involved wherever she could. She stayed either at the farmhouse or the cottage. She was not afraid of getting her hands dirty and loved working with the animals. They grew fond of her and looked forward to her visits. Stephen had little time to spare, but he had met her parents who were happy for their daughter to spend her time with him. They understood she wanted to be with him at the farm near the lake and fells. Her mother missed having her around but accepted her daughter was moving on to another stage in her life and it was time to let her go.

The day arrived for the ewes to be returned to the fields close to the farm for lambing and at breakfast time Stephen asked, 'Who's visiting Ted today?'

Muriel said, 'I am as you and your father are on the fell bringing the sheep down, and I know your mother is busy. I'll visit this afternoon then go into town to do some shopping, have tea out somewhere, and then go back for an early evening visit. That will save two journeys in one day. Just be careful up on the fell - we don't want a repeat of last time the ewes were brought down. I don't think any of us could go through that again.'

'Don't worry it's a lovely morning and Dad and I are well prepared for the job. It's not as though we aren't used to the fells. I'm really excited to have the opportunity to do this as I'm not sure Ted would ever have allowed just the two of us up there if he had been fit and well. I expect he'll spend the day fretting about it but I'm determined to prove that I'm capable of running things until he gets back on his feet again.'

'I'm sure you'll do that. The work you've done without Ted is amazing and you always work hard.'

'It's all in a day's work. I just had to get on with it and use a bit of common sense when Dad was not around. We're taking Tess and Meg with us again but I can't wait to start taking Tia as well. I reckon if we were to take her now she would just run wild and distress the ewes which would be a disaster. All in good time - we'll start to train her properly soon, and as Zoe has already said she would like to help I've suggested we start together with just a few sheep in the field. One thing I don't think she will master is the whistle as she's already tried several times and not a sound comes out so she ends up in fits of laughter. You've probably noticed she's very fond of Cass and I think she's her favourite as she fusses over her more than any of the other dogs.'

'We all have our favourites don't we. Ted can't wait to see Tess again.' They finished breakfast and Mark arrived on time. They went across the field to the truck with Tess and Meg. Stephen said he would ring Zoe at the hospital to let Muriel and Ted know when the ewes were safely off the fell. Mark said, 'Ted's mind will then be at rest and he won't be worrying.'

Muriel left the house not long after to do her morning jobs outdoors before she tidied the house until it was time to get ready for her visit. She never tired of visiting Ted as every day she could see a slight improvement and she encouraged him to keep pressing on. She hadn't thought that Ted would be in hospital for such a long time but nobody grumbled as they looked forward to his return home.

Muriel had grown close to Sheila and her family, and they cheerfully shared the work on the farm. The year passed quickly and lambing time had been and gone when the doctors at last said that Ted could possibly make it home in time for shearing. He was delighted, but warned he would need a wheelchair for mobility outside for many more months, along with crutches to help him around the house.

The doctor warned, 'This is going to be a long job and it cannot be rushed, so you had better prepare yourself for that.' The doctor knew it could take up to a year for Ted to be fully mobile again.

'I don't care what I have to use as long as I can get out of here,' Ted said his tone sounded as though he had served a long prison sentence rather than being nursed back to health. 'Telling me I'm able to see my wife back at home with my dogs, sheep, and everything I have lived and worked for, will be the best thing to get me out of this bed, walking and working again.'

Muriel cautioned, 'Don't be getting too excited as there's still a long way to go. There are certain things I need to sort out at home to be sure everything is safe for you to move around.' He listened to her with a cheeking grin and said, 'Yes, but I will have my own part-time qualified private nurse when I get home.'

He talked about Zoe and how lucky they were to have her in their lives. She had spent more and more time at the farm. Muriel rebuked him, 'Just you be careful what you're saying. She's Stephen's girlfriend not your private nurse.'

'I know, but from what I hear they seem to spend most of their time at the farm rather than the cottage so I guess we'll be having permanent lodgers at home and, you know what Muriel, I think I'll like that.'

'We'll see, perhaps Stephen will move back with his parents when you return home. What we do know is that he's welcome to stay wherever he wishes and Sheila has got used to him not being around all the time so she probably won't mind. With Zoe staying at the farm when she's not working it would make more sense for them to stay with us as we have the extra rooms. But Ted, our priority is getting you home first and then decisions can made be after that.'

They marked the days off the calendar for Ted's expected return when what Muriel had dreaded happened. A delivery van came to the farm with a large parcel and after a brief chat Muriel signed for it, not noticing that Tess was loose in the yard and had run behind the vehicle. As the driver reversed she heard a yelp. She waved frantically at him pointing to the rear of the van. He had felt something and had also heard the yelping. He switched the engine off, leapt out and ran to see what had happened. The dog's front left leg was trapped under the wheel and, by a miracle, her body had been missed but it was obvious she was badly injured. Muriel, in tears, knelt down to watch as the driver got back in his van and inch by inch moved the vehicle forward and freed her leg.

Stephen was working nearby that morning and heard the yelping. He offered to drive Muriel and Tess to the vets immediately. The driver was upset about the accident but had no choice other than to continue with his deliveries that morning. He promised to ring to see how she was. Muriel reassured him it wasn't his fault and Tess should have been in the barn with the other dogs. She telephoned the vet to let them know they were coming and what had happened. Using an old rug they carefully moved Tess on to the back seat of the car. Muriel sat beside her to stroke her and make sure she didn't move. Her early years of study and working in the vets came flashing back to her and she remained fairly calm, reassuring Tess that she was going to be alright.

'How are we ever going to tell Ted this has happened?' she asked Stephen her voice trembling at the thought of giving him more bad news.

'We don't. I suggest we keep it from him until we find out what her injuries are and what will happen. We can't tell if there are any internal injuries. The wheel could have hit her body - we can't know for sure.'

It was obvious surgery would have to be carried out as Tess's leg was crushed from the weight of the vehicle, but it seemed she had only grazed parts of her face and body. They were confident she would survive.

When they arrived at the vets Simon Forbes took Tess straight through to X-ray. After an anxious wait he returned with the results. 'I'm sorry Mrs. Thornton, but we are going to have to amputate. The leg is badly damaged but there doesn't seem to be any internal injuries. She's still young, and well enough to survive the operation. We'll start immediately so if you would just like to leave her with us we'll ring you later to let you know how she is.'

Forbes Mason and Partners had been the farm's veterinary surgeons for many years and Muriel knew Tess was in good hands. Muriel was due to visit Ted in the afternoon but Stephen thought it wasn't a good idea.

He said, 'I'll go instead. There's nothing spoiling at the farm this afternoon and I'll think of an excuse as to why you couldn't make it. Ted will believe me because you hardly miss a visit unless you have a genuine reason. We'll decide later how and when we tell him about Tess when we know exactly how she is. I can't see any sense in upsetting him.'

'You're right. There's no point in causing him unnecessary worry when we are trying to get him home. You could say that I had forgotten I had a dental check-up today.'

'Sounds a good idea. Only I don't want you going in tonight either as you're nearly sure to give it away. I know how hard it is for you to keep anything from him. He would start worrying about where he's going to get another sheepdog and the time it takes to train a good one.'

'You know me well, don't you? We'll think of something before then and, for his health's sake, I don't need to mention Tess.'

'No problem, we'll head back to the farm and I'll get changed and make my way up there. Everything will be fine you'll see.'

CHAPTER TWENTY TWO

Ted was due home in time for sheep shearing in early summer. He was overjoyed at the prospect, even though he would be in a wheel-chair for a long time and using crutches around the house.

'I don't mind if I have to leave here strapped to this bed,' he told the doctor on receiving the news. 'As long as I can leave hospital and return to the farm I don't care what equipment I have to take with me. How soon do you think it will be? Have you got a date in mind so I can let Muriel know as soon as possible?'

He was excited about the prospect of being at home with his wife, seeing his sheep, dogs, and the familiar landscape. He was keen to say a proper thank you to Tess as he believed she had helped save his life. He was convinced that if she had not raced down the fell to let Mark and Stephen know there was something wrong, he would never have sur-vived if he had been left lying injured in such terrible conditions. Muriel thought it better not to tell him about Tess's accident fearing he might blame her for leaving her unattended in the yard. Tess was going to make a good recovery and, by the time Ted was home, the vet said she would be running on three legs as well as she had done on four.

The date for Ted coming home was arranged for June and plans were made to make him as comfortable as possible. Everything necessary for easy wheelchair access was ready by the end of May and a small party was arranged for those who had helped out while Ted was in hospital. Zoe's parents were invited as they had met Ted in hospital. Close friends were involved with the homecoming plans. Muriel and Sheila baked in advance, while Stephen and Zoe arranged 'Welcome Home' banners and balloons to decorate the farmyard and house. They bought some drinks and arranged for Ted's favourite music to be played. They knew Ted would tire easily and wouldn't be allowed alcohol, so were keeping the welcome home event small and friendly.

Muriel was excited on the morning he was expected home. Stephen was up early to attend to everything on the farm and Zoe, having arrived the night before, helped set everything out in the dining room. Laughing, Muriel said, 'If this room could talk it would be asking me what is so special about today, as you've found a use for me at last.'

Puzzled Zoe asked, 'Do you not use this room very often?'

'Hardly ever, we're always too busy, and the kitchen table is big enough for our needs. We don't come in here often but there couldn't be a better reason to use it than Ted's homecoming. I really can't wait to have him home again.'

'I bet you can't, and you know, we'll all still be here to help as it won't be easy when he first comes home.'

'We're so lucky that you and Stephen met. Everyone is happy for you both and are hoping that you two will share your future together.'

'Oh I don't know about that Muriel. It's early days yet, but we do get along very well. Now enough chatting let's start setting the table or before we know it you and Mark will be heading off to bring Ted home.'

Muriel gave a little squeal, as she wrapped her arms around herself like a child overcome with excitement.

'Anybody there?' Sheila shouted from the empty kitchen.

'We're in the dining room, come through, the more the merrier.' The atmosphere was electric and the women felt this was going to turn out to be one of their happiest days for a long time.

'It's like Christmas without the presents,' Muriel laughed.

'Well remember we did say we would have Christmas when Ted came home,' Sheila reminded her.

'He's our best present today, and he comes already unwrapped!'

They all laughed and the morning seemed to go quickly. When Stephen returned, they reluctantly stopped to join him for coffee. They needed to discuss what to do about Tess when Ted arrived home.

Sheila suggested, 'Tess needs to be in her usual place, fastened up in the barn with Meg. It's going to be a slow process lifting him out and into the wheelchair until we get used to it, and if she spots him she might forget her training and jump up.'

'Well I think Meg and Tess should be shut up as usual then, when we hear the car coming up the lane, I'll go into the barn and wait until Ted is safely in the wheelchair,' then, she hesitated for a moment. They wondered what Zoe was going to suggest next. She continued, 'With Muriel and Mark at either side of the wheelchair, ask Ted to whistle for her and as soon as he does I'll free her and she will run so fast towards him at first he won't even notice her leg is missing. With both of you right beside him, if she gets too excited you'll be able to control her and we can all watch as man and dog are reunited.'

'What a brilliant idea Zoe,' Stephen said, then added, 'I always knew there was a reason I had to bring you to Felix Hill Farm, but I was never sure what it was - now I know!'

Zoe lightly tapped her hand on his arm, 'Well, even if that's all you need me here for Stephen, at least it was for a very good cause.' They smiled at one another knowing how much their relationship meant. It was obvious how much they cared for each other.

'That sounds a good idea to me too,' agreed Sheila.

Muriel added, 'I would never have thought of that Zoe and, once he's seen that Tess can run and jump about the same as she did before he'll be fine. He understands animals and will know that she will be almost as fast as before.'

They continued getting the house and food ready for Ted's arrival. When it was time for Muriel to get changed to go and collect him she left the remaining preparations to Sheila and Zoe. Mark arrived to go with her at 1 o'clock. The plan was Ted would be ready when they arrived, and they would leave the hospital at around 2pm. They would be back at the farm around 3pm by which time the guests would have arrived and be in the dining room ready for Ted. If he didn't feel up to the welcome, the guests had been warned.

Mark drove to the hospital as Muriel felt a little apprehensive even though she had longed for this day to come. When they arrived Ted was already dressed waiting with his bags packed, Muriel hugged and joked, 'Well it's nice to see you dressed for a change Ted.'

'Aye, and all new gear at that. I reckon these nurses won't want me to leave looking so fine and dandy.'

'Who's this smart fellow then?' the physiotherapist asked as she popped into the ward to say goodbye.

'I bet you never reckoned on me looking this smart when I'm all dressed up for a night on the town!' he said chuckling.

'Listen don't you be going out there and chasing the women yet, you have a long way to go before you can start doing that.'

'I won't be chasing any women. I have the only woman I have ever wanted in my life right here with me, and I might be in a wheelchair but I can promise her this, one day I will walk again and I will make her the happiest woman.'

'I'm already the happiest woman in Cumbria. Taking you home with me today, nothing could top that,' Muriel said. 'Come on then let's be getting you home.'

Some of the nursing staff came to say goodbye and he found it quite emotional, but promised them that whenever he could he would return to see them all again. He knew this was not his final visit to the hospital as follow up appointments for check-ups and physiotherapy were already made. Leaving the ward Muriel pushed the wheelchair to the lift while Mark carried his case. Downstairs, porters waited until Muriel brought the car to the door where they helped Ted into the back seat before lifting the folded wheelchair and crutches into the boot. Meanwhile Mark stayed in the foyer out of sight and rang Sheila to tell her they should arrive home at approximately 3.15pm.

Mark drove carefully and all three chattered for the whole the journey, and once they turned onto the Howtown road, Muriel sensed that Ted's heart was racing.

'Keep calm Ted, we don't want you getting over excited and having to take you straight back to hospital.'

'I'm okay, I just can't believe Mark is taking me back to the farm that I love so much. It seems so long since I walked these fields and fells.'

'It is a long time Ted, almost seven months but you will see that between us we have managed to keep things going.'

Passing the place where Michael was brought ashore, Ted leaned forward and put his hand gently on Muriel's shoulder. She knew what his gesture meant, and without speaking stroked his hand in acknowledgment. Michael was never far from their thoughts wherever they were, but there were certain places along the road that were reminders of that tragic day. Not wanting to forget how much coming home meant to Ted, Muriel pointed out what a beautiful summer's day it was.

'You'll have to be careful in the sun. It's a long time since you even breathed fresh air let alone felt the sun on your skin.'

'I can't wait, as soon as I get into my wheelchair one of you can push me over the yard to see the animals and have a look at everything.'

'You're in for a pleasant surprise when we reach the lane, and there will be no outside inspection today that's for sure.' Muriel kept her thoughts to herself as they passed Felix Cottage.

'Sheila at home is she Mark?' Ted asked.

'She was earlier but I'm not sure now,' Mark said evasively.

Muriel found it hard not to give the game away. 'Zoe's here too but I think she was going looking for a new outfit today. She said you'll be tired tonight but they'll be coming to see you this evening and she and Stephen will stay overnight with us to be there should I need any help.'

Mark added, 'I think you'll need a bit of help for a while, and Stephen has already said he intends to carry on living at the farm if it's okay with you.'

'That lad's welcome to anything after all he's done for us.'

Mark turned slowly into the lane and Ted noticed all the decorationss hanging across the farmhouse. He was stuck for words. He tried again, 'Whose idea was this or need I ask?' As they approached the front door he saw Sheila.

'You didn't expect us to bring you home without a welcome surely?'

'I don't know what I expected but it certainly wasn't this.'

Mark stopped the car and Sheila waved from inside the door, not wanting to make a fuss as there would be excitement enough for him to face over the next couple of days. Lifting the wheelchair from the car Mark fumbled as he tried to open it up safely. 'You just sit there Ted until we're sure this thing's safe for you to sit in.'

'I'm going nowhere fast Mark. I've made it back to the farm so there's no reason for me to have to race through the door immediately. I want to admire the view for a few moments anyway before I go inside.'

Everything was going to plan, then Ted asked, 'Where are the dogs? In the barn I hope?'

'They are Ted. We decided to keep them safely out of your way until you were ready for them. As soon as you're ready you'll see them. I expect you want to go round the sheep even more. There are a few in the pasture so we'll take you over there soon.'

It wasn't easy getting Ted out of the car and into the wheelchair but with careful handling they managed.

'Now take a bit of time to get your breath back and look at what Stephen and Zoe have done to decorate the house.' Muriel was determined she was not going to rush things. Growing impatient as he would have to be wheeled to see the ewes, Ted asked for the dogs.

'Zoe will let them out, she's round there with them. You give a whistle and they'll come.' Ted hardly had time to whistle before the dogs came running towards him, and sat wagging their tails in front of him. He gave them both a pat, and it wasn't until Tess moved around that he realised her leg was missing.

'What on earth happened to her? And why didn't you tell me?'

Mark said, 'Muriel didn't want to worry you. Getting you well and back to the farm was more important. We knew she would recover in time for you coming home. Just look at her, she's a walking miracle, no she's a running miracle, and as we expected you didn't noticed anything as she ran towards you.'

'To be honest I didn't but what happened?'

'We'll tell you all about that later. Let's get you indoors and welcome you home properly.'

Mark took the dogs back to the barn to be shut in safely and Muriel pushed the wheelchair up the new ramp and into the kitchen. Sheila heard them come in and had popped into the dining room to let Ted's close family from Newcastle and his best friends know he was on his way. As Muriel pushed the door open Ted was greeted with a chorus of 'For he's a jolly good fellow.'

'My word what a welcome home...' He took Muriel's arm and kissed her hand and said, 'it's wonderful to be back.'

The guests welcomed him one by one and Ted beamed with happiness. 'Let's not let this good food go to waste - help yourselves.'

Once the guests were all talking and eating he asked Muriel to take him back across to see the sheep and lambs. As they crossed the yard he said, 'You can let the dogs out for a minute too.' He patted them as they sat by the wheelchair and he gazed over the fields, wondering how long it would be until he could walk again.

Returning to the farmhouse, he said a few words of thanks to his family and friends, especially Muriel and Stephen, before everyone left. Sheila and Zoe volunteered to clear the dishes while Mark and Stephen offered to help Ted upstairs.

'Not before we all have a drink to celebrate around the kitchen table, my favourite place,' said Ted.

They agreed it had been a wonderful day and chatted happily about all the things that had happened in the last few months. Mark and Stephen saw Ted safely upstairs while the dining room and kitchen were tidied. Muriel went to bed, leaving Stephen and Zoe alone downstairs.

'Looks like history is repeating itself,' Ted said happily to Muriel, his mind thinking back to their younger days when they were left alone with Jack upstairs in bed.

'Goodnight my love, it's lovely to be home again.'

'Goodnight Ted, it's lovely to have you home, sleep well.'

Chapter Twenty Three

The months that followed saw few changes for Ted. He was able to move around parts of the house where he could easily reach for something to hold on to without his crutches, it was not easy, but he insisted on trying and progressed gradually.

He said to Muriel, 'If I don't try I will never throw these damn things away, and I promised you the day I left the hospital that one day I will walk on my own again.'

Muriel remembered but sometimes wondered if he would ever succeed. Zoe explained that he was improving and that they both had to have patience as they were expecting too much too soon. There were times when Ted would become frustrated but he reminded himself that the alternative could have been paralysis or even death, which instantly cheered him up, and he tried again. He accepted that he would need his wheelchair for some time to come, but told himself the day would arrive when it, along with the crutches, would not be needed.

Life was easier for Muriel without having to visit the hospital. She was able to help Stephen around the farm as well as do her other jobs. She took Ted in the wheelchair over the yard to see what was going on, and he helped with tasks like holding the hose and filling the water containers, filling the cat and dog bowls, washing and boxing eggs, anything that could be reached from his chair. These tasks helped boost his morale and encouraged him to keep battling on.

Sheila and Mark's life returned to normal. They visited Ted and sometimes took him out for the day. Muriel wanted Ted to be within sight, but knew it was good for him to get out and about as they would take him down to Pooley Bridge to chat to people. Everyone was friendly and said they looked forward to the day when they saw him without his wheelchair. Stephen lived between two homes, that of his parents and his employers. He enjoyed this because nobody seemed to mind where he stayed. If Zoe was free they would stay at the farm, but would regularly visit Sheila and Mark who were now enjoying the prospect of having a daughter-in-law. The young people seemed so well matched, and spent all their spare time together. Zoe continued working as a nurse, but loved being at the farm. She told Stephen her first interest would always be nursing, but she loved the outdoors, especially the sheepdogs and enjoyed working with Cass.

Tess had become completely adapted to her three legs and tourists were amazed by her agility. Zoe had joined a web forum for three-legged dogs and spent some evenings at the computer chatting online with different dog owners. They were surprised at how many there were, and came up with the idea of introducing a new fun class at Penrith's annual agricultural show.

Zoe asked if anyone would be interested in a three-legged dog race at the show and she was delighted at how many people were keen to enter their dogs. Surprised by the response Zoe said she would ask the show secretary for a new class or a one off fun run to be included in the next show. Ted was keen for them to try. He'd allowed himself to become a bit sentimental and Tess was more than just a working dog to him.

'Let's not get too carried away,' said Stephen, 'as they might not agree to it yet.' Zoe was in touch with the show secretary who said the idea would have to be put before the committee, discussed and voted on. The letter said that, as Ted had become well known locally, and had entered his sheep in the show for a few years, there might be a possibility that the vote would be in favour. It wasn't a proper agricultural class, but it would please children and pet dog owners, so it would be put forward.

The show committee made a decision in favour of the new class. The secretary's letter said that, as the family at Felix Hill Farm had been through so much in the past few years, and Ted was still confined to his wheelchair, the committee had agreed to allow the event to take place for one year only in the main ring just before the grand parade. They would allow two heats if there were enough entries, with first and second from each heat going into a final race.

Everyone at Felix Hill Farm and Felix Cottage was delighted at the news. Stephen and Zoe set about making the arrangements, explaining on the web forum that they could take up to four dogs for each heat and, as Tess was entering, this left only seven free places. They filled the places quickly and, sent off the official entry forms to be completed and passed on to the secretary. They planned everything for the new class hoping that nothing would go wrong as they were excited about the new event.

The day of the show arrived with perfect weather which attracted the crowds to see one of the finest agricultural shows in the country. Through the programmes and the press, word had spread about the dog fun run and people looked forward to seeing it. Muriel and helpers went along for the day so Ted could enjoy the show as he had missed the previous year's event. Zoe's parents were there and they took it in turns to make sure Ted was comfortable and able to watch as many of the classes as possible, and to view the livestock and trade stands. He met people he hadn't seen for almost a year and enjoyed a chat with them.

Towards the end of the afternoon an announcement came over the loudspeakers, 'All entries for the three-legged dog race please make your way to the main ring.' Stephen and Zoe were already at the ringside ready to lay out the ropes to mark the lanes along with a couple of people who had volunteered to help. Two others would be at the end of the 50 yard run to judge first and second places.

The ringside was crowded as the day drew to a close. The grand finale attracted hundreds of spectators. Ted, Muriel, Mark, Sheila and Zoe's parents didn't want to miss one second of the event and had taken their positions near where the race would end and the winning owner would be presented with a small trophy. The excitement grew as they watched the first four dogs waiting to start the race, and the crowds clapped as they waited. A short sharp whistle and the dogs were set free, racing towards their owners who were shouting their names willing them to run as fast as possible. It was a close heat between first and second but there was no disputing the third and fourth places. The owners were delighted, patting their pets with pride and giving them treats.

The second heat was about to begin, Stephen held Tess and whispered, 'You can do it lass, you can do it.' The whistle blew and they were off. The shouting at the other end was deafening. A boxer beat Tess by a head, but at least she was in the final.

The final was held back for about ten minutes to give the second race dogs a fair advantage by giving them a short rest. When the dogs returned to the starting line the crowds were clapping and whistling. Stephen's heart was racing, and the second he let go of Tess he was off himself to the finishing line. People shouted, 'Come on Tess, come on,' and 40 yards into the race she overtook the boxer by a head to cross the winning line first. Ted's family and friends jumped, clapped and shouted, 'Well done Tess we knew you could do it!' They were overjoyed at the success.

Simon Forbes, Tess's veterinary surgeon had volunteered to present the trophy to the winning owner, and he was pleased to be presenting it to Stephen and Zoe on Ted's behalf. Shaking their hands he began talking into the loud speaker. 'I'm sure everyone here will agree it has been an absolute pleasure to watch these paralympic dogs take on this challenge and, although there can only be one overall winner, I'm sure you'll all agree not one of them failed. They have all done their owners proud and they're all winners. Tess ran that race like greased lightning and I am going to sign her winner's certificate, 'Tess, Cumbria's three feet of lightning.' The crowd cheered and holding the trophy he asked Stephen and Zoe, 'Will you collect this trophy on Ted's behalf?'

'No they won't. I'll collect it myself,' a voice from behind announced. Ted walked towards them unaided, took the trophy in his hand and lifted it above his head. People who knew him explained to their neighbours in the crowd what had happened and he was given a standing ovation. The crowd clapped and shouted until their hands and throats hurt. Stephen turned to Zoe and quietly said, 'That's fantastic he will be able to walk with me down the aisle as my best man at our wedding.' She hugged him so tight he knew he had the answer he wanted, but today for them the highlight was Tess, 'Three feet of Lightning and the man who walked again - Ted.'